D1664074

Prizm Books

Aisling: Book I Guardian by Carole Cummings
Aisling: Book II Dream by Carole Cummings
Aisling: Book III Beloved Son by Carole Cummings
Changing Jamie by Dakota Chase
City/Country by Nicky Gray
Climbing the Date Palm by Shira Glassman
Comfort Me by Louis Flint Ceci
Desmond and Garrick Book I by Hayden Thorne
Desmond and Garrick Book II by Hayden Thorne
Devilwood Lane by Lucia Moreno Velo
Don't Ask by Laura Hughes
The Dybbuk's Mirror by Alisse Lee Goldenberg
Echo by Amanda Clay
Foxhart by A.R. Jarvis
Heart Sense by KL Richardsson
Heart Song by KL Richardsson
I Kiss Girls by Gina Harris
Love of the Hunter by V.L. Locey
Josef Jaeger by Jere' M. Fishback
Just for Kicks by Racheal Renwick
The Next Competitor by K. P. Kincaid
Repeating History: The Eye of Ra by Dakota Chase
The Second Mango by Shira Glassman
A Strange Place in Time by Alyx J. Shaw
The Strings of the Violin by Alisse Lee Goldenberg
The Eye of Ra by Dakota Chase
Tartaros by Voss Foster
The Tenth Man by Tamara Sheehan
Tyler Buckspan by Jere' M. Fishback
Under the Willow by Kari Jo Spear
Vampirism and You! by Missouri Dalton
The Water Seekers by Michelle Rode
Eagle Peak by Elizabeth Fontaine

Lunaside

J.L. Douglas

Prizm Books an imprint of Torquere Press Publishers
P.O. Box 37, Waldo, AR 71770.
Lunaside Copyright © 2015 by J.L. Douglas
Cover illustration by BSClay
Published with permission
ISBN: 978-1-61040-860-8
PRINT ISBN: 978-1-61040-869-1
www.torquerepress.com

First Torquere Press Printing: January 2015
Printed in the USA

www.prizmbooks.com

Dedication:

For Elizabeth, who is magic.

Lunaside
By J.L. Douglas

Chapter One

If you saw me right now, sitting here as I am on the tallest and greatest dune on all of Trundle Island, with my strangely overdressed and very small girlfriend resting her head in my lap, you'd probably think a couple of things.

First, you might recognize me from TV. I never thought being a silent helper on a cooking show could make someone a celebrity, but life keeps proving me wrong on that.

Last fall and again this spring, I was roped into being my semi-well-known gourmet-chef father's on-screen assistant on his cooking show, *Tastes of Trundle Island*. It meant giving up almost every weekend of the school year, but Dad really wanted me to do it, so I decided to go for it.

I actually get asked for my autograph occasionally, which is totally awkward. But I haven't been invited to do any more episodes, so I'm hoping my minor fame will fade soon enough.

The other thing you might notice is how totally cool I seem with just lounging on the dune with my girlfriend, like there's nothing better than spending time with her out here in the open where anyone could see us.

You might see me like that and say, "Wow, now there's a girl who's proud of who she is. She's so confident."

You might say that, but you'd be entirely wrong. And you wouldn't see me in the first place, because the past seventeen years have taught me that no one ever comes to my dune. No one but me and, more recently, my girlfriend.

On the off chance you did see me, you still might wonder if I was from TV, but confident? No way.

In fact, I did see a guy coming down the path just a few seconds ago. He didn't look familiar and was likely one of the tourists who stayed at the resort down the road from my house. He wasn't even looking at us, just strolling around, probably. But I still reacted.

I shoved Andrea off my lap, accidentally sending her rolling down the dune a little. When she resumed her previous position, she frowned. "I get that this is still probably weird for you, being out in a place where every single person has known you since before you were born. But, like, maybe try *not* reacting next time?"

"Mm, okay." I make a token effort to run my hand through Andrea's short, dark brown, heavily cowlicked hair, hoping to seem at least halfway okay with this.

She hums with satisfaction, then pulls her phone out of her black dress pants and starts checking it. "Yeah, sorry. I'm just on edge, I guess. As much as I'd like to, I can't spend all of July and August sitting on the dune with you. Don't get me wrong, it's great and all, but what'd really complete this summer is—"

"Finding a film job for a few months," I recite, finishing the sentence I've heard a million times since we started seeing each other. "To finally get some paid experience working on a film set. Also, money to buy me presents."

"Shut up," she giggles, before slipping the phone back into her pocket. "There's nothing wrong with wanting to get a head start on my career."

"Maybe not, but you've still got a year of high school left!"

"That's easy for you to say," Andrea groans, whipping out her phone again and listlessly running her fingers over its surface. "You've been on TV, and you're set for your dream summer job. By the time *you* go to university, your CV will be downright imposing."

"Okay, but I barely know what a CV is, and university isn't exactly on my radar yet. Oh, and working at Lunaside isn't my dream summer job," I say, but I can't help grinning because it actually is.

Last summer, I got hired as a counselor for Art Camp at Lunaside, a little summer camp down the road from my house. I loved it, and not just because it was so close to home. I'd wanted to go back but was too shy to ask to be rehired.

But then in late May, Madeline Jarre, the owner, called me up to say, "So, I'm hoping you're going to tell me you're willing to be my head counselor for Art Camp. Of course, we only ended up with five enrollments, so you'll effectively *be* Art Camp. Do you think you can do that?"

I told her I could definitely do that.

Andrea slaps my leg. "Oh, whatever, you're in heaven."

"Guilty." I wince, not wanting to gloat.

"Don't feel bad about it! You're awesome," she says, grabbing my hand and squeezing it. "So what if you've got more experience in your field—and also mine—than I've got in film? Basking in your reflected glow is still pretty great."

"I do not have more experience in your field than you," I protest.

"Keep telling yourself that, superstar," she jokes. "If it wasn't for *Tastes of Trundle Island*, we'd never have met!"

She's right about that, at least.

I met Andrea during one of the spring tapings of Dad's show. Apparently she'd developed a crush on me from watching the first batch of episodes. Then she used her mother's connections as the producer of our show to visit the set. Creepy as that was, we hit it off and she kept coming back to our filming sessions. Not long after that, I learned Andrea Grey is not the kind of girl who messes around. Thanks to Dad accidentally outing me on set with some casual joke about how I had a crush on the camera girl, Andrea asked me out during her fifth visit to the set.

I guess being on TV made me sort of bold, because somehow I decided to risk my security and said yes. She'd wisely decided that our first date was going to happen at the beach we were now overlooking. That went well; we kissed—she initiated—and then we listened to our hearts after that, I guess.

"I helped my dad hold boxes of strawberries and bowls and stuff. I am so *not* a superstar."

She sits up, finally resting her phone in the sand after checking it another three times, and looks me in the eye. "Maybe not, but you're still my superstar," she breathes in her husky yet high-pitched voice that kind of makes her sound like a really mousy jazz singer.

At that second, I notice someone else coming down the path—an older lady in a really loud orange sweater—and swat Andrea in the arm.

"You dork!" I say, hoping that'd make her get off me so I won't risk rolling her down the dune again.

She raises an eyebrow, still looking half-ready to bury me in kisses where everyone can see. "Huh?"

"I'm talking about your corny line!" I joke, hoping to hide my incredibly mixed feelings about our apparently impending make-out without upsetting her.

On the one hand, Andrea is a fantastic kisser. My experience is admittedly limited, but kissing her is like having a rainbow explode in my head while getting a full-body massage. Just the thought of that feeling sometimes makes me want to wrap my arms around her and push her into the sand and forget my shyness and the guys walking down the path and just everything.

On the other hand, there is my shyness and the guys walking down the path and just everything.

She pulls away from me with a wounded look and

immediately starts checking her phone. "Oh. Sorry. I just—I got carried away."

I put my arm on her shoulder. She does not shrug it away.

That doesn't mean my stomach hasn't turned into cement with guilt, though. It does that every time I pull away from her like the neurotic ball of neuroses that I am, just because she might have given some random person the impression that we're a couple.

Me being me, I just can't understand her need to be so incredibly open about us. I'm really shy about stuff like that. And by that I mean I'd rather fall into a bottomless pit than admit I have a personal life.

"It's okay," I try to reassure her, but it comes out sounding pathetic and like a lie.

Sometimes I wish I could tell her that my weirdness is because I'm still getting used to people reacting to me being out, but it isn't. I've been pretty lucky in that way, because everyone who matters to me has been pretty supportive.

Well, everyone except Mom.

At first, she seemed more okay with it than Dad or my brother. They just made good-natured jokes about it, but she teared up and gave me hugs and talked a lot about how parents should love their children unconditionally.

That reaction made me feel all fuzzy and accepted, and it wasn't until I invited Andrea home for dinner that I realized this "should" applied to Mom, because her love was definitely conditional.

After the dinner, which I thought had gone well, Mom kept me at the table and lectured me over tea. Apparently I'm using this "gay crisis" as an excuse to keep from experiencing life or something, just because I'm heading for senior year without showing any interest at all in going to university.

I wanted to point out that it was kind of ironic how she rejected Andrea right away, when she's the upward-climbing daughter Mom probably always wanted to have, but I don't really do conflict. We haven't said much to each other since.

That makes living together pretty awkward, but I'm hoping that really rocking this counselor job and keeping my relationship with Andrea going will show her that I *am* living my life. I just don't care about CVs and five-year plans.

I rub Andrea's back in an attempt to be comforting. "Any luck with that dream job?"

"No one's e-mailed me back, and it's mid-June. If I don't hear something soon, this summer's going to involve a whole lot of me sitting on the couch, watching *Tastes of Trundle Island* reruns while you teach adorable little kids how to do art."

"We shot twelve episodes. That's hardly enough to get you through a whole summer," I tease. "Also, I'm sure there's a job out there for you. You're in film—don't they just hire people randomly for, like, a couple of weeks at a time? I'm sure you could check one of your, uh, film people websites and see if you could help out on the set of some cheesy black-and-white movie about people staring at sunsets or—What? I don't watch movies. But maybe do that?"

"Yeah, maybe. I guess that'd be better than nothing."

While she goes back to checking her phone, I let my mind drift. I've gotten to imagining myself sleeping on the warm sand, listening to the breeze blowing through the marram grass that grows all over my dune, getting tingles at the back of my neck, when Andrea yells, "Moira! Oh my God! Did you—How come you didn't tell me about this?"

"Huh? What? What didn't I tell you?"

"Lunaside has a Film Camp! Did you know about this?"

"There wasn't one last year, and Madeline just hired me back over the phone this year, so—"

She grabs my shoulders and squeals. "Ah! You know what this means? I've gotta get—I'll need to polish up my

CV, make sure everything's set to go on my demo reel..."
she trails off dreamily. "I should—I should probably go
now, huh?" she says, biting her lip as if that is the only thing
that can stop her from exploding with glee. "I'll talk to you
later?"

I force a smile. I really want to be happy for her and
definitely don't want to begrudge her a potential job at the
greatest summer camp in the world. But assuming she gets
hired, this complicates my general plan for showing Mom
that I'm a pretty competent person overall.

Because even if I'm not girl-crazy like she thinks, there's
definitely a chance that working directly with my girlfriend
will make running a summer camp on my own harder than it
already is.

Chapter Two

I go to sleep without any contact from Andrea and wake up the next morning to the same. But that doesn't bother me. She's probably perfecting her demo or constantly rewording her CV before sending it or slaving away at her cover letter or something. And loving it.

When I sit down at the kitchen table, I check my phone a few more times before starting in on my breakfast. Then, after another quick glance at my phone, I throw open the huge picture window beside the table.

Now *this* is a morning. The sun is casting an orange, early-morning glow over our yard, while a lazy haze drifts over the grass, forming a thin, low-hanging cloud that foretells summery warmth. And that salty, earthy scent that I like to pretend can only come from a Trundle Island morning is so strong that it pretty much overrides the taste of my usual bowl of vegan granola, which I guess is pretty bland to begin with.

I decide to leave breakfast half-finished. This just isn't a morning for sitting around, staring at the view. Whether or not I hear from Andrea, I need to *do* something.

***

My itchy feet lead me to Lunaside, just in front of the vinyl-sided "cabins" that Madeline had installed especially for us counselors. She'd apparently done that so she could pull from a more varied pool of talent, rather than only hiring people who, like me, just live down the road.

I head toward the front of the cabin that belonged to Bailey—my former co-counselor and now one of my best friends—and me last summer. Then I sit down in front of it, crossing my legs, and closing my eyes.

The grass is still a little wet, which complicates life for the white-and-green ivy-print sundress I'd chosen to wear that morning. But that's a minor inconvenience for this clean, untouched moment of tranquil aloneness that I'll never get once camp starts.

But then some psycho in a red car whips through the Lunaside field, almost running me over before dropping off his or her passenger, so I sort of forget my good mood.

Almost immediately, the car's former occupant heads over to me—a decidedly curvy girl, roughly my age, with jet-black, ear-length hair, and eyes so faintly colored that they're basically white. She's more striking than pretty, but she catches my attention anyway.

"So hey, sorry about scaring the crap out of you," she declares with a nervous laugh, apparently not noticing that I might have been staring at her.

"It's okay," I reply. "I guess I shouldn't have been randomly sitting on the ground this early."

She half smiles. "You a counselor here?"

"Mm-hmm," I hum. "I do Art Camp."

The girl's ghost eyes brighten. "Oh, so *you're* Moira? Layla's told me about you."

Layla? While I find our head Drama counselor sort of goofily charming, we barely know each other. All I know about her is that she's the manager's daughter and a theatre student at some university somewhere. All she knows about me is that I like art and, thanks to me coming out to the camp last summer, girls.

I guess I don't have to wonder too hard which of those things makes for interesting tales to attract new counselors.

"I'm Millie. I'm helping her out this year."

"Yeah?"

"Yep. I'm pretty psyched to be working here. Summer camps tend to draw in people like us, but I've never gotten the chance before. Heh, chalk that up to having no discernible talent in anything, probably."

People like us? I'm pretty sure I know what she means, but it's surreal to hear it just thrown out there like that.

In my life, there's really been no "us." Since last summer it's mostly just been me, occasionally facing down family friends and neighbors who either strongly disapproved of my sexuality or held me up like an exotic specimen—the Rare Endangered Lesbian Cooking Show Assistant.

My only "us" has been Andrea. And even then, her situation's a little different. She's basically always been out, which means she's had to face a lot more real-world attention for it than I have. Because of that, she just sees her sexuality as a natural part of herself. There's really nothing political about her, and I kind of find that refreshing.

When I first considered the possibility that I might be dateable to some girl somewhere, I worried that I'd have to learn all these obscure terms and signals and stuff before I'd be allowed to find a partner. Meeting Andrea was great, because she eased my fears of being shown up as the ignorant country girl from an island in the middle of nowhere that I am.

"Right, um, well, I hope you have fun?" I cough.

"Heh, I'll try."

There's a second where we both go quiet until Millie laughs again. "So, listen, I gotta unpack. Maybe we'll catch up later?"

"Maybe," I mouth.

She answers with a quiet chuckle and then heads toward the cabins.

***

After my run-in with Millie, I pull my phone out of my bag and check it again. When I see nothing from Andrea, I head for the cafeteria, figuring I'll grab a snack or something.

Just as I enter the cafeteria, someone yells, "Hey!" from somewhere unseen.

I search for the source of the voice and see Layla, looking as goofy as ever in a neon orange t-shirt with a cartoon triceratops on it, jogging toward me from behind the cafeteria stage.

"I'd like it very much if I could give you a hug," she states, with a totally sober expression that makes me laugh.

When I tell her she can hug me, she springs forward and wraps me up in a professional yet warm squeeze that makes me wonder if she runs a hugging booth at university.

She holds me at shoulder length and smiles. "You're looking great! That's not to say you weren't before, but you look... peaceful," she says with a knowing look.

"Huh," I mutter. Peaceful is not usually something I feel, especially not with people around.

She pulls her arms back but then rests a hand on my shoulder. "Well, I've gotta get back to taking inventory of props and costumes. Mom says we've got a bit of extra money this year, so I have to see if there's anything we might need to buy. Plus, we've apparently got Bailey on board as our costume designer, so who knows what we'll come up with."

I nod. Bailey had squealed that story to me over the phone a few weeks ago. Her grandmother had dropped her as my co-counselor because of the whole "only five campers" thing and also the fact that Bailey's no artist. Then Madeline flat-out rejected her idea for a Fashion Camp on the grounds that no one would go.

Eventually Luna, Layla's mom, suggested hiring her back as Drama Camp's costume designer instead of as a counselor. Madeline agreed that this was the perfect workaround to avoid firing her granddaughter. And Bailey, who tends to prefer fabric to people, pretty much literally jumped at the opportunity.

"You'll have to meet my new assistant at some point," says Layla, looking me in the eye.

"New assistant? You mean Millie?"

She furrows her thin-yet-untrimmed eyebrows. "Yeah! Do you know her?"

I shake my head. "I saw her come in this morning. She got dropped off by some psycho in a red car."

She grins. "Aside from the poor driving skills, Randy's a great guy! He actually lives here on Trundle Island year round."

"Huh, I don't meet too many island drivers," I comment. Trundle Island can't exactly brag about its high amount of paved roads.

"No? Anyway, you two should definitely hang out! She's new to the island, and I think she'd like spending some time with someone who knows her way around. Plus, only having me for company has probably driven her half-insane by now," she whispers, even though we're the only counselors in the cafeteria.

So there it is again. Layla has apparently told Millie about me. Now she wants us to hang out. Is Millie some kind of screwed-up social reject who needs Layla to orchestrate friendships for her? Is she just secretly a huge fan of *Tastes of Trundle Island* and desperately wants my autograph? Is it something to do with Millie's opinion that "people like us" tend to grab summer camp jobs?

I give Layla no indication that I want to hang out with Millie at any point, but she smiles as if we've already set a time. "Okay, well, you have a great day, Moira! Take care."

"Yeah, you too."

As Layla skips back toward the stage, I start to change my mind about hanging out in the cafeteria. Who knows when Millie will appear from backstage, ready to "catch up" like she'd said? As much as I wanted to do something this morning, it'll no doubt be safer for me if I just head back home for now.

When I push through the double doors, I see that the sun is much higher now and grayish clouds have moved in. And not the ones that foreshadow wild, black thunderclouds, either, just boring old smoky clouds that aren't really anything. As I head down the path and away from Lunaside, I take a pathetic pleasure in imagining that those clouds mirror how I feel right now.

I'd woken up to an orange sky, with a quiet, ethereal haze drifting over my surroundings. Now everything is just gray and bland.

I keep staring up at those stupid clouds as I walk. Part of me wants those wild, black thunderclouds to descend on me right now, while I'm walking home.

Part of me wants to see lightning.

Chapter Three

Andrea calls me the next day to tell me she got the job, and I'm happy for the distraction.

Sometime in the midmorning, I'd picked up my sketchbook and started drawing a circle, then two lines meeting in a cross at the center of it. A few idle scribbles here and there. More circles; two of them just above the horizontal line. Other details, more lines here and there until my drawing was no longer a random mess of circles and lines.

Before long, it became something else. Something that scared me a little because of what it probably meant. This drawing had become a face; an incomplete face, with a slightly crooked nose and small lips and eyes in a color I wasn't even sure had a matching shade in my collection of markers, but a face nonetheless.

When my phone buzzes from somewhere on my floor, I toss my sketchbook aside with a relieved sigh. "Hey?"

"Hi! Sorry about not calling earlier. They hired me shortly after the interview, but Mom took me out to dinner to celebrate my getting the job, and you know how stuff like that goes."

"Yeah," I reply, although I really don't. "So I went up to Lunaside yesterday," I blurt, hoping to turn the subject away from Andrea's relatively healthy relationship with her mother. "I caught up with Layla, and I almost got run over by the guy who dropped off her assistant. The assistant's name is Millie, and she—Well, I just get the feeling that everyone's pretty psyched to get started with camp."

And probably they are. Just because Millie's the only one who literally said that doesn't mean the rest aren't thinking it.

"Yeah!" chirps Andrea. "I can't wait! Actually, though, do you think that maybe we could both walk up later today? I'm excited to meet everyone, but I think it'd be less awkward if you introduced me."

"Um, well, I can do that, I guess," I reply.

"Great!" she squeaks. "So, can I come over now?"

I look over at my now-closed drawing book. "I'd like that, yeah."

"Okay, I'll rush! I should be about a half hour. I still have to get dressed and fix my hair and stuff."

I have to laugh. Andrea's hair is plagued with cowlicks at the best of times, and lately she's grown it out a little. So now she's got this adorable-in-its-awkwardness style that's short on the back, with long bangs that she sweeps off to the left. That means that no amount of combing or hair gel keeps it from looking like she just rolled out of bed. But I like it. It's accidentally cute, like mostly everything else about her.

"Andrea, your hair can't be fixed. You know it's going to look the same no matter what."

"I know," she whines, "but that doesn't stop me from waking up every morning with hope."

"Afternoon, you mean. Anyway, I'll be waiting."

"Okay, I'll go as fast as I can. See you soon!"

"All right, bye," I reply, resolving to keep my drawing book closed while I wait.

***

I'm about halfway through what is probably my fifth cup

of tea of the day when Andrea knocks on my door. Just once, like she always does.

"Hey," I say, smiling at the fact that she's decided not to wear a sweater vest for once. Instead, she's gone for a blue polo shirt, which shows off her impossibly bony arms, gray slacks that look unintentionally baggy, and freshly shined black dress shoes. In other words, she looks even more like a skinny nerd than usual.

Without thinking, I pull her into the house and kiss her a bit more eagerly than I'm expecting. Because apparently "skinny nerd" translates to "sexy" in my language.

"Wow, where did that come from?" She grins.

I tell her it's just because she looks great, which is half-true. I leave out the part where I'm distracting myself from what I'd drawn this morning. Because I'm just not sure what will happen when I meet the drawing's inspiration again.

***

Bailey is the first person we find. She apparently caught an afternoon ferry to the island and is now sitting on the step of the cabin we'd shared last year. When she notices me, she waves.

"Moira!" she sings, running up to me with her arms outstretched.

We hug for like a second before she pulls away. Bailey's all ambition and no follow-through when it comes to hugs. As if she only realizes she actually doesn't like them at the last minute.

"And you are looking fabulous, by the way!" she exclaims, grabbing my hands before reaching out and running her finger through a loose strand of curls that has draped itself over my shoulder. "Mm, your hair! Such shiny, perfect hair is absolutely wasted on someone who cares so little about it, but it's still wonderful."

"Uh, thanks. You look great too," I reply with less enthusiasm. Even though looking heart-stoppingly gorgeous is kind of Bailey's thing, she really doesn't know how to take compliments. Today she has on a black tank top with some illegible gold cursive design, black Capri pants, and a pair of matching flats. Her brown hair is tied back in a high ponytail, and she's wearing black feather earrings, along with a couple of gold bangles. Kind of dressed down from her usual, but I have a feeling that these are Bailey's "work clothes."

"Huh, yeah, thanks." She shrugs before turning her eyes on Andrea and making a weird little half-smile. "So you're Andrea, huh?"

"Yep!" She nods.

Bailey raises her eyebrow while smiling and holding her hand over Andrea's head quizzically, like she's wondering if my girlfriend is tall enough to ride the roller coaster. "Okay, so you are the cutest thing I have ever seen. I want to put you in my pocket and take you home. And I absolutely *adore* the androgynous metro-meets-country-club thing you've got going on."

"Thanks!" replies Andrea with a smile.

Bailey shoots me a funny look I can't interpret. "Okay, sorry to run, but I've got to get back to helping Layla put together the materials for this year's set of costumes! Still pretty excited about that, by the way."

I smile. "I'm sure you are."

"Yeah. Oh, and Moira? Grandma gave me your key for our cabin. I'll get that to you later, okay?"

"Oh?" I hadn't really thought about how sleeping arrangements would work until that moment.

"Did you really think she'd place you with your girlfriend? Anyway, she gave me first pick and I'm selfish, so I look forward to bunking with you again, cabinmate! That's cool with you, right?"

"Of course."

"Fabulous. So, I'll catch you later, Moira?"

I nod.

With that, Bailey heads back into our cabin, grabs a black book, closes the door, and heads toward the cafeteria.

She does not say she'll catch Andrea later.

Seeing as Bailey lacks people skills at the best of times, I write that off as awkwardness and go looking for the other counselors. We end up catching Jeremy, Andrea's co-counselor for Film Camp, on his way out of his cabin. Apparently he's not heading anywhere in particular but just doesn't want to be the loser hanging out in his cabin and playing video games all day.

Since he was Layla's co-counselor last year, he and I spend a few minutes catching up on life. We never really got to know each other that well, but we bonded one morning after I'd come out to my fellow counselors. The two of us were having breakfast alone, and he told me about his older sister's coming out, which was when I started to get a bit more confidence that I wouldn't end up alone forever.

I formally introduce him to my girlfriend, but she does the rest. In less than a minute, she's squealing about the kinds of film activities she foresees the campers liking, while Jeremy just nods kindly.

Andrea had probably begun preparing a point-by-point plan for this camp seconds after she was hired. Jeremy, laid-back as he seems, likely hasn't listed more than a few notes even now that camp is a few days away. They are meant for each other.

The downside is that he invites her into his cabin for a meeting. When she squeezes my hand and invites me along, I tell her I'd just get in the way and also be bored to sleep by all that film talk. She accepts that with a grin, exuberant at finally getting down to business.

Unfortunately, it also leaves me standing alone in front of the cabins. Just like yesterday morning.

Since it's evening, the camp should be buzzing by now. I expect to see Jude—my best friend, who applied to the camp so we could spend our summers together in spite of having jobs—or maybe Rory, taking a break from planning Sports Camp to tease me about how I have nothing planned for my camp yet. But the whole place is totally silent and dead.

Then I feel that unmistakable feeling of someone standing behind me, and suddenly it isn't.

I turn around. It's Millie.

She greets me with a little wave. "Hey there."

"Uh, hi."

She smiles sort of sleepily. "I was hoping I'd find you. Layla said you were the girl to ask if I wanted to see the sights of Trundle Island."

I chuckle. "Oh yeah?"

"Yeah, she says you're from here?"

"Born and raised."

"Wow, I'll bet *that* wasn't easy, huh?"

I shrug. "It wasn't so bad."

"Right. Layla said you're kind of in love with this place."

"And she's right," I find myself saying.

"So, uh, do you feel like giving me a tour right now? Maybe not the grand tour. Just a... mini-tour? I'm looking for a good place I can go to clear my head. I think a lot, you know?"

"A mini-tour," I mouth, feeling dazed and stunned and really not in control of my words.

"Heh, so you wanna lead the way?"

I mumble something that I guess tells her yes, because soon enough Millie and I are heading away from Lunaside and on our way to the beach. We don't stop at the dune, but she doesn't need to be told to take her flip-flops off as we walk along its path to get to the beach.

We sit on the shore and at first just watch the gray clouds that haven't left since the morning and the waves. The sea is pretty calm today, just a quietly lapping tide that makes for pretty inoffensive background noise.

"So, yeah," Millie starts, her voice sounding hoarse, "I guess Layla's told you all about my situation, huh?"

"Um, well? She and I aren't actually that close."

She laughs as if she understands. "Yeah. We weren't that close, either. But we go to the same university, and we're both members of our school's gay-straight alliance."

So *that's* why Layla insisted that we hang out. It doesn't explain everything, though. Does she just feel like I'm better equipped to talk to Millie about this stuff? Is her little childlike heart fluttering at the thought of setting up a couple of her gay co-counselors?

I shift away from Millie a little. In case that's her intention, I don't want her getting any ideas.

"She's sort of a boss in the group. She's asexual, and apparently she started going so she could stop feeling so invisible and to get tips on how to explain her sexuality to people. Dealing with that inspired her to stick around and help out other people in the group. So she got trained as a volunteer counselor in the same space. She rules. Like, when people come out to their families and stuff, she always makes sure they're safe."

"Huh, that's really cool," I muse. And here I've been thinking of Layla as this grown-up four-year-old who mysteriously manages to hack it in the real world. Endearingly silly, but maybe not much more than that.

"Yeah, well, anyway, I spent two whole semesters going to the group and working up the courage to tell my parents. By April, I'd gotten brave enough to go for it. But then I told them, and things kinda crashed down on me. Turns out, they were super against it. I figured they'd be cool because they're not, like, religious or anything and that's where the horror stories always came from in our group. But yeah, Mom told me it was a phase, and Dad called me a 'pervert.'

Heh, as if anyone says that anymore. Anyway, they kicked me out until I'm 'over it.' Then Layla called me up the next day to see if I was safe. I told her I wasn't."

"Oh," I whisper, suddenly feeling sympathetic for this girl. No doubt she's just reaching out to me because, in her mind, I'm some kind of kindred spirit. Somehow, that isn't so threatening. And I guess I can sort of relate. Mom hasn't kicked me out, but she isn't exactly happy with things as they are, either.

"Yeah, so Layla got her mom to get me into Lunaside so I wouldn't be at risk this summer. Then my brother Randy came and got me as soon as he heard what happened. He lives on the island. Mom and Dad look down on him because he's in construction and they're both academics—math professors, actually—so he keeps his distance. Now I guess I'm just figuring stuff out as I go."

"Wow," I breathe.

She chuckles and stares out across the waves. "I was really looking forward to meeting you, Moira. We've got lots of girls in our group who are out, but, like, most of them are big-city types. But when Layla told me your story, I pictured you as this tough-as-diamonds butch. Like you'd have a motorcycle or something. I just pictured the kind of girl who could come out in a place like this and deflect all the ignorance."

"I've never even been on a motorcycle," I reply with a little chuckle.

"My point exactly. Guess what I'm trying to say is that I came here expecting some inoffensive role model type who'd be like my surrogate sister for the summer so that I could get my life back on track."

The waves keep up their quiet lap, lap, lapping, even though I'm willing them to be a bit more enthusiastic. Right now, I need a roaring tide to drown out this conversation. Better yet, a tidal wave to wash me away so I don't have to face it.

After I fumble something like a sentence, Millie turns her ghost eyes on me. "I was *not* expecting you."

Chapter Four

In spite of all the excitement of seeing the counselors, and all the good feelings it gives me about starting a new year at Lunaside, it doesn't take me long to get bored of planning my own camp alone. Saturday afternoon, I text Andrea.

Hey, I'm at home. Wanna plan camps together?

Her response is immediate.

Of course! Just w/Jeremy right now! Invite him along?

I can't help but laugh. Andrea Grey, the world's youngest workaholic.

No Jeremy, please. Might want to do other stuff.

Within a half second, she replies.

Will be there in five.

Her "five" feels a lot shorter than that. In what has to be like three minutes at the most, she's on my doorstep, knocking her gentle, single knock.

When I go to let her in, I immediately give up on the whole "planning camps" facade. Andrea has shown up in a purple Lunaside t-shirt and black soccer shorts that show off her small, yet definitely existent, shape. Besides, I'm really stuck with what to do for Art Camp anyway.

I lead her into my room, making sure to close the door tightly. Mom doesn't see therapy clients in her home office on Saturdays, but she also doesn't leave the house if she can help it. Mostly that means she holes up in her room and reads novels all day, but I don't want to risk a run-in.

Andrea kisses me a little as we move toward my bed and drop onto it. It's not exactly steamy love-scene material, but it's all I can manage. I want more than that, obviously, but I just can't shut off my brain. What *if* Mom barges in on us? Would she use this moment as proof that I'm a do-nothing loser who lives exclusively to lure girls to my bedroom?

Eventually I just give up entirely.

I sigh as I roll away from Andrea, feeling kind of defeated and like I don't deserve to be kissed right now. "I *really* want to, Andrea. It's just that—"

But she just rolls back into me and rests her head on my shoulder. "You know I'm always willing to take things slow. You *are* my first girlfriend. It's not like I even know what I'm doing most of the time."

In a second, my neuroses melt and I wrap her in my arms. It's not easy remembering that we're both figuring this out as we go along. Sort of, anyway. While I'm just feeling my way through things, I know my girlfriend's got a list somewhere of all the things she plans to do with me. No doubt she's probably called it something adorable like "Things I Hope to Do with My Girlfriend (Moira)."

"That's good, because I don't, either," I mutter.

She grins. "And I am very thankful that I get to profit off that."

"What?"

She meets my eyes. "Um, you're stunning? And if you ever figure out just how amazing you are, you'll realize how many girls are checking you out and my time will be up!"

I drop a pillow onto her face. "Oh, be quiet! Statistically speaking? You're the only girl on the planet who'd ever notice me. Because you are weird."

Part of me has sort of started believing that this isn't actually true, thanks to that awkward moment on the beach with Millie, but it's still weird. I'm definitely not used to anyone talking about me like I'm a physically desirable human being. And not because of low self-esteem. I think I look okay, but being reminded that I have a body bothers me. Like somehow there'll come a time when I'm floating off into my own world of euphoria, and then I'll think, *Oh right. I'm not an ethereal being of pure light and happiness*, and crash back into the real world.

Andrea gives a long sigh and sprawls her arms and legs on top of me. "Whatever, it's just such a relief to have a job for the summer!"

"I think you are the only person in all of history to say that," I point out, happy she's wisely left that other topic behind.

"Shut up," she giggles. "I just—Ah! I don't know who I am when I'm unemployed. My whole life's been scheduled since I was six, and I've been hanging out on the sets of Mom's shows since I was like twelve. Free time kind of breaks my brain, you know?"

"I really don't," I reply, giving her a playful shove.

She rolls her eyes. "Right. Hippie. You wouldn't understand."

Hippie. That's probably a good word for how I feel about the whole "having a job" thing. I'm not a slacker. I just don't feel the pressure to stack my CV so that I can get into the best university when I don't even know why I'd be going.

"Too bad Mom doesn't see it that way," I grumble. "In her world, not caring about future studies is a mental illness."

Andrea puts her arm around me and kisses my ear. "She's probably just stunned that her awesome, brilliantly creative daughter has no desire to do anything with that."

"I don't know if it's that. Right now, she literally thinks my life goal is to make out with girls."

Andrea chuckles and moves her head towards my neck. "Aw, well, I can definitely think of worse life goals."

I shiver at the feeling of her lips touching my bare skin.

"Not helping."

"Who said I was trying to help?"

"Mm, true," I sigh, exhaling as I let loose a little and try to enjoy this.

And it does feel good. The sensation of Andrea kissing my neck, ears, and eventually lips while her small hands caress my bare shoulders transports me somewhere beyond my mother's ridiculous plans for me. Somewhere dreamy. Somewhere comforting. A room made of a comfy old sweater—euphoric, cozy.

It almost makes me feel like I can let go of my stupid neuroses and reciprocate. Maybe, after all, I can be a real girlfriend and not just a paranoid, guilt-ridden lump on the bed.

But that's not happening. Just as I wrap my arms around Andrea's waist, someone knocks on my door.

I silently hope it's Rory. No doubt he'll make some stupid joke about how he made himself some veggie burgers but forgot how gross they were and now they're mine because he has trouble just doing nice things for me. We'll laugh and then head into the kitchen. No love scene, but no big deal.

Of course, it's not my brother. When I open the door, I see Mom standing there for some reason. She's in her sapphire-blue, oversized "day-off" sweater, with her arms hanging awkwardly at her sides like she got kidnapped and dropped off at my door without warning.

"Uh, hi, Mom?"

"Hi, Moira. I had some free time this morning, so I went online and looked up some universities that you might be interested in checking out. Maybe we could go over them together later?"

"Maybe, but I'd really like to just worry about planning my camp right now."

She folds her arms and fixes her eyes on Andrea. "And I'm sure you are doing a *substantial* amount of that."

I guess she has a point. I started with the best of intentions, but actually having Andrea in my room got the better of me.

Still, I can't let her see that she's right. I look over at Andrea and call, "Hey Andrea, do you want to grab my drawing book? It should be on the floor, maybe under that pile of dirty socks?"

Eventually she finds it, dutifully gives it to me, and then wisely heads back to the bed.

I hand it to Mom. "I'm trying out potential activities myself, to get a feel for whether or not my campers might like them. Since I only have five this year, I'm looking for activities that will allow for a bit more independent drawing time."

She flips through the book that I really do intend to eventually use to practice activities, and fixates on the sketch I did of Millie. She frowns at it, and then looks at me. "You're such a talented artist, Moira."

I bite my lip. That statement cuts much more than if she'd just outright said, "If you weren't such a girl-crazy waste of space, you could really make something of yourself." Sure, I'm not exactly shooting for the stars like Andrea, but that's no reason to blame my sexuality. Swallowing down the lump in my throat, I take back my drawing book. "If you don't mind, Mom, I'd like to get back to planning my camp. Because I really *do* care about making it a success."

"If you say so, Moira." She nods and heads back across the hall, disappearing into her bedroom.

I turn to Andrea with an apologetic frown, but she smiles. "Your mom's really trying."

"Are you serious?"

She nods firmly. "Educated parents just think that education is the path to success. My mom's like that too. Part of why I'm so obsessed with getting ahead before actually going to university is because of the pressure she's put on me. Mom makes it seem like if I *don't* build up my CV, get in touch with my future instructors, and build a relationship with them before going to school, I will never go anywhere in life. Because the world is so competitive and so on."

"If you didn't, though, would she blame the fact that you like girls?"

Andrea shrugs. "No, she'd call me lazy. I think your mom's just desperately seeking for some reason as to why you're not totally jazzed about picking a top university and spending all of senior year courting it so they'll take you. And, well, this is the thing that kinda stands out."

I laugh. "It's too bad she hates you so much, considering how much you *love* her!"

"I've spent a lot of time hanging out with smart, highly successful women. They all kind of want the same thing for their daughters. They feel like the path to success is tough, and they know it's better to get into something while you're young. It's not that unreasonable, even if your mom's way of explaining your situation is pretty awful."

"She's right, though," I admit, flipping through my drawing book. "I really suck at planning stuff. Like, I invited you over to help me plan my camp, and look what happened!"

"Hey, it isn't too late," Andrea soothes. "There's still time to put together a very respectable camp and show Philoméne that you mean business."

I wonder if she might be right. Even if I do make the decision to go to school someday, it isn't all that likely that Mom and I will ever excitedly bond over it. But getting Andrea to help me make Art Camp a resounding success would be a win all around. She'll see how awesome and driven my girlfriend is, and she'll realize that I'm a pretty competent person, despite my lack of a post-secondary-education fetish.

"Okay, do your thing!" I exclaim. "Help me make my

camp sparkle. Like, for real this time."

Andrea nods. "I can do that. What do you have so far?"

Almost automatically, I hand her my drawing book. "Honestly? I've just been sketching. I thought maybe it would help me think of something, but so far—"

"Wait, she looks familiar," my girlfriend states, examining the sketch of Millie just as Mom had done.

My throat closes over with a sudden lump of anxiety. "H-huh?"

"This drawing. This is that Drama counselor, isn't it? Millie?"

Cold drops of pure nervousness form on the back of my neck. "Uh, well?"

"You really captured her eyes. I had no idea how... striking they were. I guess I never really thought about it, but she's actually really good-looking, isn't she?"

At that moment, the only sound I can make that half-passes for a response is a weak, strangled, "I guess."

Chapter Five

Come Monday morning, camp starts. When Bailey suggests that we do breakfast at the cafeteria as soon as it opens at six, I immediately agree. First days aren't for sleeping in.

But I soon regret that.

After I grab a vegan muesli cookie and a tea, I sit beside Bailey. Almost immediately, she blurts, "Millie's so hot."

I choke. Bits of half-chewed cookie splatter across the table. Appetizing. "I'm sorry, what?"

Bailey sips her coffee and nods toward the stage. Millie, who is apparently also an early riser, is currently there sorting what appears to be a bunch of random junk—hairbrushes, golf clubs, a mailbox, a bag of feathers, a few dolls, and other things that look like they were raided from someone's garbage—into neat lines. I assume these things are part of Drama Camp's prop collection.

She has on a gray version of our camp's t-shirt, dark skinny jeans, and a pair of black flip-flops. A bit less striking than our first meeting, but not enough to make Bailey wrong.

Millie is *definitely* hot.

Bailey smiles, still watching her. "She's just really got it going on. I'm a little in love with her look, and maybe kinda jealous. Did you know she's in English Lit? I mean, really. Where does an English Lit student get that kind of style?"

"I really have no idea," I say, staring at my half-eaten

cookie.

Bailey elbows me, and then juts her chin in Millie's direction. "I've seen you checking her out."

"What? When?"

She just winks. "Hey, I'm not judging. If I was into girls, she'd be at the top of my list." Then she turns toward me with a grim expression before cracking up. "Uh, yeah, sorry. I don't date close friends."

"Oh."

"I just think you two would make a cute couple," she muses. "Millie's way cooler, but she's also a pretty deep thinker, so she'd likely get you. Plus, you're both a nine out of ten on my attractiveness scale—the only one that counts. Well, Millie is. You'd be a nine if you'd shower and wear clean clothes more often."

"Shut up," I mutter. "And haven't you been paying attention? I have a girlfriend."

She pushes her lips to the side of her face and gulps her coffee. "Huh, yeah, I guess you do."

"So, enough about this, okay?"

"Yeah, okay. I'm just being stupid," Bailey admits.

"Yes. Very," I reply.

"Still, you didn't say you weren't into her," she points out.

I gulp down my breakfast and politely tell my friend to have a good first day of costume designing before heading outside. Not that I mean it.

Stupid Bailey. Even if she'd been talking about Andrea, I'd still be unsettled. Talking about people in such a sexual way has just always unnerved me. It doesn't do justice to the person's whole self.

And, okay, I'm just mad that she's not only figured out my feelings for Millie already, but also supports them entirely.

The thought ties my stomach in guilty knots. Andrea

thought Millie was good-looking too, but she hadn't reduced it to such a carnal label. Because that's just not what she's like. Andrea is cutely G-rated in that way. She feels attractions like most people do, but she feels no need to make them all about the sexual side of things.

Remembering that makes me smile and fills me with the urge to head toward the cabin Andrea shares with Jude. Since Jude is likely off doing her early-morning beach sprints, I know my girlfriend probably has the cabin to herself. She's also probably still deep in sleep, but that's unimportant.

As soon as I step into her cabin, I go over to her bed and remorselessly shake her until she starts making groggy almost-awake noises.

"Ah, M-Moira?" she groans, staring at me with half-open eyes.

"Good morning!" I sing, kissing her on the forehead and then squeezing her tightly.

"Huh, well, I like that."

"Yes, well, you can't have it again unless you wake up," I tease. "So get up, get dressed, and maybe we'll get a couple of minutes together before our campers run us off our feet!"

"A couple of minutes?" she scoffs. "It can't be later than seven o'clock. Camp starts at nine."

"Yes, but *drop-off* starts at eight! I know you're new to the whole camp thing, but most parents cannot wait to drop their kids off at the earliest possible second. So, up!" When she finally rises, I tap her playfully on the butt.

With a stunned glance at me, she rushes to grab the clothes she carefully laid on the wooden storage box at the foot of her bed the night before: a soft pink sweater vest, a white polo shirt, and black pleated dress pants. Evidently her obsessive need to look her best has clashed with the camp's fairly relaxed uniform.

Feeling like I need to do something to absolve the guilt I feel from this morning's chat with Bailey, I put my arms behind my head as Andrea gets changed and make it really obvious that I'm staring at her. I sigh a lot and raise my eyebrows as I watch. Whistling would add to the effect, but I don't know how and now isn't the time to practice.

While I'm usually too hung up to do something totally normal like that, it's pretty easy once I have an excuse. Beneath the stuffy outfits, Andrea's so delicately pretty that even if I didn't know her, I'd still instinctively want to wrap her up in my arms forever. That I know she's got an impossibly sweet, nerdy little personality to match just gives me this feeling of all-encompassing warmth, like standing on a hill on a blazingly sunny mid-July afternoon.

No, she probably doesn't even register on Bailey's scale of attractiveness. Bailey wouldn't call her hot. But Andrea is pretty and accidentally adorable and very attentive to my stupid needs.

Better yet, she's *mine*.

After she's carefully adjusted her sweater vest so that its V lines up perfectly with the button line of her polo shirt, I get up, wrap my arms around her, walk her back to the bed, and then kiss her longer than our usual. "You're wonderful."

She raises an eyebrow but smiles. "Okay, seriously, what did you have for breakfast?" Then she wrinkles her nose and adds, "Well, I guess I know what you had for breakfast because you always eat the same thing. But still."

"Quiet, you goof," I giggle as I kiss her again.

As usual, we go no further than a few kisses. A combination of just wanting to be with Andrea and wanting to purge the guilt of my attraction to Millie overrides my anxiety for once, but the real world soon makes itself known again.

I hear a loud knock, then look toward the cabin door's square window and see Jeremy, who seems to have his back to us. Did he knocked on the door like that, just to be polite? I decide that he had, just because it makes me like him even more than I already do.

"Come in!" yells Andrea.

The head of Film Camp sheepishly pokes his head inside. He explains that he only wants to let Andrea know that some of the kids have already shown up, even though it's still fifteen minutes before drop-off time. He doesn't want to interrupt, of course, but he thought he'd let her know.

Andrea sings back, "Don't worry! I'll be right there!"

Once she leaves to join Jeremy, I go and grab my Art Camp materials from my cabin. After all, I don't have a giant, friendly nerd in a Lunaside t-shirt to warn me when my campers are arriving.

***

When all five of my campers have seated themselves on the patch of grass just outside my cabin that'll be Art Camp's non-rainy-day home base, I hand them each a drawing book. After I do that, I invite each of them to tell me a little about themselves, hoping that I can divine a fun first activity out of their stories. One that is preferably both awesome and instructional. Instructional I can do, but a straight lecture about line art would put the group to sleep pretty quickly.

First up is a mousy-looking girl named Allie, whom I recognize from last year. The way she jumps when I call on her isn't encouraging, but I hope for the best.

"Well, I love comic strips," she admits, her eyes widening. "I don't even care what it is. Funny strips, family dramas, mystery stories, goofy superhero adventures—if it's got a story told in four panels, I am *there*."

She pushes her hair back and then smiles a little. "Right now, I'm working on one. It's just about my life and my misadventures. I guess I'd like to learn how to make it better? And I'd like to show people for once. Oh, and maybe give it a title? Yeah, those would be my goals—Wait, we were even supposed to have goals?" she asks, pulling at strands of her frizzy, almost-black, waist-length hair.

I smile both because I love when kids are interested in art and because of the potential activities I can siphon from her response. But I resist that urge for now and invite the camper beside her—a bulky, pale girl I don't recognize, with wide, blue eyes and a mushroom cut—to share her interests.

It takes her a second to realize I'm calling on her, but eventually she nods at me and says, "I came here to work on my specimen drawings. See, I'm super into bugs, and I keep a sketchbook of all the different species I see. Except my sketches are kind of bad. The eyes are a big problem for me, but sometimes I get a leg wrong or, like, I miss a wing—it's kinda frustrating. So, yep, if you can help me with that, I'll be your biggest fan forever."

I nod. "Life drawing is one of my specialties, so I think we can work with that. But, hmm... I don't think I remember you from last year. What was your name?"

"Right!" The girl laughs. "Yeah, yeah, names—I forget little details like that when I'm thinking about bugs. Uh, I'm Emma, but people at my school call me 'Bug Girl' and I'm totally cool with that too. Oh, and I just wanted to add that I think another goal of mine would be to learn how to draw a perfect cockroach. See, they're my favorite bug. I hope that doesn't gross anyone out, because I'm pretty in love with them."

I scan the group for disgusted faces, but none of the other campers really react to her admission at all. Possibly because they've never seen a cockroach. Here on Trundle Island, they're basically a myth.

The scrawny boy sitting next to Emma confesses that he has no idea what a cockroach looks like but that he thinks insects are cool. He then goes on to tell us about a superhero he'd created, called Centipede Man, admitting that he only got as far as giving him "centipede powers" before abandoning his creation.

"So, yeah, my name's Terrence," he continues, "and all I'd like is to finish a project for once. Like maybe a short comic or something? Just something I could show my dad and my friends back home."

I assure Terrence that we'll figure something out, while inviting the stocky boy next to him—whom I recognize as Neil, one of my star artists from last year—to introduce himself and pad my activities-idea list some more.

What Neil says isn't that much of a surprise. He's really into drawing ocean scenes, especially waves, and he's kind of a kindred spirit for that. For him, it's because he's always out on the water with his parents—his dad is a marine archeologist, and his mom is a marine biologist. But I assume the basic idea is the same.

I open my mouth to welcome Neil back, and tell him how hard it really is to draw a wave properly, when the small, blonde, denim-clad girl between Neil and me shouts, "I'm next, right?"

I sigh. This girl is a returning Lunasider too. But last summer she was so loud and obnoxious and openly critical of my somewhat relaxed counseling style that seeing her now is a surprise.

"I'm Shapiro Hanley," she explains, looking at each group member in turn before staring at me in disbelief. "I don't really have any goals, but I just wanted to say... I saw your show, Moira."

I raise an eyebrow. "You mean—?"

"*Tastes of Trundle Island*, yeah. Dad watches it sometimes. He was trying to be a better cook for a while, but since vacation started he's kind of given up. He goes out every night and leaves me with babysitters."

I stare at her, unsure of how to react to that frank admission.

"So, hey, where's Bailey?" she asks, looking around.

Even though she took great pains last summer to remind Bailey that she was a terrible artist, Shapiro apparently looked up to her and even went through a phase where she wore black all the time because that's what Bailey does. And she never stopped reminding me that, even though I can draw, I'll never be as cool as my co-counselor.

"Bailey's around. We only needed one art counselor this year, so she's the costume designer for Drama Camp."

Shapiro nods. "Uh-huh. That's probably better for her. I thought it was stupid that she was in art."

As I struggle to follow that up with some kind of response, she continues with, "So, um, do you think I could go see Bailey now?"

I start explaining that Bailey is pretty busy with planning costumes for Drama Camp, and how we might see her at lunch, when suddenly I am hit with a wave of inspiration.

"Everyone," I say, with a little hushed awe at my sudden flash of brilliance, "would you like to draw your goals? Shapiro, you can draw Bailey."

While everyone else is getting into their projects, she retorts with, "Nah, I'd rather draw you," before adding, "but that was smooth how you used us to get out of thinking of anything yourself."

But soon even she gets to work, which makes me feel pretty confident in my ability to run a summer camp on my own.

***

By the end of the day, everyone has finished working on their drawings and seems mostly satisfied with their work—even though Shapiro is the only camper who shares what she's drawn.

"Hey, Moira!" she yells, waving her drawing book around. "I'm done!" She presses her lips together and frowns. "So I really tried to draw you. But, argh, you're just so obnoxiously tall that unless you have some mural paper or something, it's a lost cause."

I stare at the page. She certainly captured the ivy print of my sundress, even making an attempt to draw textures on about half of the leaves. And the dress seems to fall in roughly the same places around my knees and chest that it does in reality. The only problem is that everything below her drawing's legs and everything above the chest extends somewhere beyond the page, leaving it headless and footless.

"Keep trying with your proportions," I encourage, "and you really seem to have a skill with textures. Maybe try drawing textures on the rest of the leaves?"

"Hmm, maybe I will," she answers, staring at her drawing.

The rest of the campers declare that they aren't ready to show me their drawings but will finish them at home. That doesn't seem all that encouraging, but when their parents start to arrive, I get to listen to the kids tell them how I'm a talented artist and an awesome counselor. Who cares if I've earned it; it's still pretty gratifying.

Soon enough, I'm down to one camper. But Shapiro's father had been late to pick her up almost every day last summer, so I'm not all that surprised to be working overtime on the first day.

When the others are gone, Shapiro grabs my hand. "I know Dad was always late last summer, but now I actually don't mind because it means I won't have to go to the babysitter yet."

"So, what's your babysitter like?" I ask, feeling a sudden pang of concern for her.

"I see a lot of different people. Dad just leaves me with whatever neighbors are around. I hate it. Last summer, we spent lots of time just barbequing on our deck or renting silly movies and making fun of them. Now he just goes out, and he doesn't even tell me why."

"He could be busy at work," I offer. "You said he's a

lawyer, right? I'm sure they work almost all the time."

"Maybe, but he usually takes time off in the summer. I just wish he'd stop being dumb and tell me why he's out all the time, or at least get me a babysitter who's not, like, two hundred years old. I wouldn't mind so much if my babysitter was just one person and, like, a teenager or something."

When her father arrives not long after that little exchange, I suddenly suspect why he's been so absent lately. Even ignoring the fact that he reeks of musky cologne that smells more expensive than pleasant, he's dressed in a dark red silk shirt that would likely make even Andrea feel overdressed. He's also gelled his blond hair up in a way that I imagine wouldn't be appropriate for any kind of evening business meeting, let alone one with lawyers.

"Aidan Hanley," he reports, "I'm here for my daughter."

Shapiro sighs loudly. "I'm right here, Dad."

He looks at her. "Oh, right. Sorry, Shapiro, but we need to go."

"I know," she says, sighing again. "We always need to go."

"I told Annie I'd drop you off at her place at five o'clock sharp. It's almost a quarter after four now, so—"

"Aw, Dad! Annie? She's always trying to get me to go outside so she can teach me how to chop wood or to carve stuff out of it or whatever. You're a lawyer, Dad—aren't there laws against making kids work like that?"

"No, Shapiro," Aidan answers.

"Well," she huffs, "she always wears plaid shirts. There must be a law against that."

Her father looks at me anxiously, then scratches his thin neck and exhales. "Annie's very good to us. She's just trying to pass on her trade because she has no kids of her own. Besides, it's an important, um, meeting and I can't—If it goes well, maybe I'll explain it to you, but for now we really need to go!"

Shapiro looks at me and says, "See you tomorrow, I guess," then follows her father across Lunaside field and into his small, shiny, black convertible.

As soon as the Hanleys leave, I kick off my sandals and sit in the grass. Then I close my eyes and remind myself that it's early summer: my favorite, most euphoria-inducing time of year.

But my journey to scenery drunkenness is halted almost immediately by the sound of someone dropping heavily to the ground. When I open my eyes to discover what kind of monster would interrupt such a transcendent moment, I see Jude. She is making a token effort to match my legs-crossed sitting pose. She soon gives up and stretches her legs outward with a laugh. "I'll never figure out how you sit like that."

"It's a very comfortable position," I reply, straightening my posture. "And I'm honestly surprised that you can't. *You're* the star rugby player. The only exercise I do is walking, and I'm flexible enough for it."

She slaps her muscular thighs. "I guess these legs aren't meant for the kumbaya scene. I'm sure I'll get over it."

I laugh.

"So anyway, I didn't come over here to learn the secret to sitting like a hippie. Me and Bailey are planning a bonfire tonight, and I just wanted to let you know because you love those things more than anyone."

"You... and Bailey?" My two best friends hadn't exactly clicked up until now. And by that, I mean Jude has no respect for fashion while Bailey thinks all jocks are boorish, mindless drones.

Jude laughs. "Heck yes. Turns out she's really into bonfires! I went to the cafeteria to grab a snack after my camp was over, and she was there having a coffee. Figured I'd say hey, be friendly and all that. Then we got to talking about how awesome it'd be to get a bonfire going down at the shore."

"That's great!" All I can picture now is Bailey getting them to wear matching bonfire-ready hoodies to celebrate their newfound friendship.

"Oh," she adds, "and your brother floated in while we were chatting and said that he was up for it too. But I was less impressed with that. Seeing how he's in love with Bailey and afraid of me."

"Rory isn't afraid of you," I answer, even though he kind of is. When we were younger, he tried to get in her way during one of her morning runs as a joke. In response, she punched him in the face, giving him a serious black eye. He forgave her, but he's never teased her since.

"Bah, I kind of like that he's afraid of me. Now that we work together, it's useful. Anyway, yeah, Bailey and I and apparently Rory, unless we can ditch him, are heading down to the convenience store in a bit to grab some firewood and snacks and stuff. We just thought we'd let all the counselors know first, so you guys can show up whenever you feel like it."

"A-all the counselors?" I gulp.

Obviously, that includes Andrea *and* Millie. And me—on my favorite beach, on a warm summer night. Somehow, I feel that Andrea plus Millie plus me plus bonfire equals disaster.

She raises a bushy eyebrow at me. "Um, yes? I know Jeremy's a geek, but he's not so in love with his video games that he's above having some fun with real people."

"Well, that's good, then." I decide to let Jude think I expected her to leave Jeremy out.

She slaps me on the back and then hops to her feet. "Yep. I think it'll be a good time. We'll hopefully catch you down there. Right now, Bailey and I are going to try to sneak off before your brother realizes we left."

"Good luck," I reply, not bothering to let her know that I

will most definitely not be catching her later.

As much as I want to go to that bonfire, especially now that Jude and Bailey are possibly bonding, I just can't. Maybe nothing would happen, but it's more likely that I would do something that'd give away how I feel about Millie. And in front of everyone.

I just can't do it.

When Andrea comes to visit me in my cabin later, interrupting my session of pathetically wallowing in guilt, I tell her I'm not going to the bonfire even before I look at her.

She immediately arrives at what would normally be the most logical reason for me to not get sand between my toes. "Aw, are you not feeling well?"

I look up. Andrea has changed into a fitted, plain black t-shirt and white shorts that go about halfway down her thighs. She's still chosen to wear these black, goofily elaborate closed-toe sandals that look like they were made for hiking, but she looks good. For once, she looks like a relaxed, regular person. It gives me the sudden urge to hop up from my bed and kiss her all over. But I don't. Because then I'd get caught up in the moment and go to the bonfire and then Millie'd be there too and things would fall apart for me or something.

"I think I have a headache," is all I say.

She sits beside me on the bed and begins stroking my hair. "I can stay with you, if you want."

I want that. That would really be the best outcome. I'd miss the bonfire, but I'd have my girlfriend here with no distractions. Still, that won't fix anything. If Andrea stays, I'll feel guilty for lying to her and also for depriving her of the bonfire.

"No, you go," I tell her.

"Are you sure?"

"Of course. I don't want to keep you from having fun. Plus, Jude and Bailey getting along is like the event of the century, so I'm going to need updates," I joke.

"Ha, well, I'll keep an eye on them," she assures me. "And you're sure you'll be okay?"

"Yeah, I'll probably just sleep or something."

"Well, if you're sure," she says, lingering only a little before she gets off my bed. Andrea cares about me, but this is a Trundle Island bonfire, after all. She kisses me on the forehead. "I'll see you later, okay? I'll head back a little early to see how you're doing."

"You're sweet." I smile.

After she leaves, I open the window over my bed and let the cool offshore breeze envelop me. It's not so great that I get over missing the bonfire, but it helps. And anyway, I did the right thing. What's one bonfire compared to that?

Except, about an hour later, I hear a knock on my door. When I see who it is, I realize that maybe I haven't done the right thing at all. It is quite possible that I have made the most wrong choice I could have made.

I lift my head and see Millie at my door. When our eyes meet, she holds up a hand to greet me. Almost automatically, I respond with a nod that I guess tells her to come in, because that's what she does.

She sits on Bailey's bed with her hands on her knees. "Wasn't expecting to see you this evening. I figured you'd be down at the beach with everyone else."

"I wasn't feeling well," I explain.

"Sorry to hear that."

"Yeah, well, it's just a headache. I'll be okay."

"Heh, well, that's good. I'm kinda glad you stayed."

I cough. "Uh, yeah?"

Millie smiles. "Definitely. I hung back because I fail at crowds, and I figured I'd be alone all evening."

"You fail at crowds?" I ask, sitting up.

She nods. "Pretty much. I'm fine with one-to-one chats like this, but get me in front of a bunch of people and all I can do is just sit there and quietly nod at things people say like an idiot. I'm just shy, but it's embarrassing."

My heart stops for a split second. So this girl is not only stunning, but possibly as shy as me? Maybe my equation doesn't need Andrea or a bonfire to become disastrous. Maybe me plus Millie is a disaster on its own.

"I know the feeling," I reply.

"Heh, that surprises me. I had you pegged as a bit of a loner, but not necessarily shy. You seem pretty cool with talking to complete strangers, anyway."

"That's different. You're a counselor. I never mind talking to counselors. I mean, we're going to be spending the whole summer together, so it's not helpful to be hung up."

"That's a pretty solid strategy," she comments.

The way she just sits there, with her hands still on her knees, tells me that she probably isn't kidding about her shyness. I hadn't noticed it until now, but maybe that's because we haven't really hung out except for that one evening on the beach. And that wasn't hanging out, because she had a purpose then—she was getting her story out there, and making sure I knew she liked me.

Now, she's just... here, and it seems like she doesn't know what to do with that.

"So Bailey says you're in English Lit?" I ask, pulling the same strategy I always wish people would use on me. Being asked about art always pulls me out of my shell.

"Yeah. I'm not sure if that's really what I want, though. Mostly I went into it because my parents are into math and my older sister's in engineering, and they're so into numbers that I just hate anything mathematical by default. I wanted to rebel, but, like, I didn't want to go for something entirely useless. But I do read a lot, so I guess it works out. And how about you? Are you in school?"

I shake my head. "Um, well, I'm actually still in high school. I'll be a senior in September. But I *was* on TV."

That's kind of a stupid thing to say, but Millie still rocks herself back a little and laughs. "Oh, man! That's wild! Were you on, like, a nature show or something?"

"I wish! But no. It was a cooking show, *Tastes of Trundle Island*. It's really my dad's show. He's a gourmet chef at the resort down the road."

"That's amazing. So are you, like, famous now or something?"

I shake my head. "The odd person asks for my autograph, but no. I don't have any movie deals in the works or anything."

"Too bad. That'd be awesome! I could see you lighting up the indie scene. You've got the right look for that."

I can't help but smile a little as I attempt to divine if that's a compliment or not. "Right look? How do you mean? I'm sorry... I don't watch a lot of movies."

Millie puts her hands together and looks through them, doing that stupid thing people do when they're pretending to be directors. "Well, first off, you've got those 'aw, shucks' red curls. And freckles! But then you're all tall and skinny and gangly, and you wear those adorable sundresses all the time. On top of that, you've got those deep, sad-looking emerald eyes. Basically, you are every indie kid's dream girl."

"Huh," I reply, stunned. Since my eyelids do kind of turn down a little, I've always thought I have sad-looking eyes. But that's the first time I've ever heard them described as positively. Even Andrea only ever compliments the color of my eyes and ignores what frames them.

"It's the truth." She nods with a laugh.

I smile. "Well, I'm sure my fans will understand that I'd rather work on my art."

"Oh, probably. There are lots of indie darlings out there." She winks. "You just keep painting or whatever."

After a pause, she leans forward and adds, "You paint, right?"

"Yes. I also do a lot of sketching."

"Nice! A double threat," she replies, sounding less impressed than she had about *Tastes of Trundle Island.*

"Uh, maybe? Anyway, do you have any talents? Or do you just do your English Lit thing 24/7?"

With a cute little shrug, she admits that she likes to write fiction in her spare time, but that mostly she does that as therapy. For a long time, she just wrote really corny girl-meets-girl stories to work stuff out in her head. She's apparently tried writing poetry too, but the results were even worse.

"I'm thinking about trying lyrics next," she jokes. "My brother Randy's an amateur country singer, and my life's basically a country song. It could be big."

After that, I start to turn the topic toward art, but Millie admits that she's totally ignorant about visual arts because of her long-standing grudge against paintings.

"Growing up, Celia and I shared a room," she explains. "And my sister was a pompous jerk even then. She covered our walls—even the ones over my bed—with prints of, like, the most obvious paintings of life. It kind of made me hate art, no offense," she admits.

I tell her it's okay and let her move on to talking about books even though I probably know as much about literature as she does about art stuff. But she doesn't seem all that interested in what I like to read and mostly takes the opportunity to talk about her interests. That's fine, though. I'm getting the impression that Millie is the kind of girl who doesn't get to talk about herself much.

She doesn't go bug-eyed about literature the way Andrea does for film stuff, but she's smiling a restrained little smile as she goes on about all the books she likes. Mostly it's just an exercise in her asking me if I've heard of this or that book, and me usually admitting I haven't but sometimes faking it and saying I have so she won't think I'm just some illiterate high school student.

"My favorite book, though," she starts, with a shamed look, "is called *The Arcadia*. Well, it's got a bunch of slightly different names, but I don't want to scare you away with my geekiness. Anyway, yeah, I had to read parts of it for a class. It's a total mess of a book—written in the fifteen hundreds, and it was finished and then it wasn't and then it sort of was again. But there was this one scene in it that hit me like it wasn't supposed to."

Apparently, the book is about these two princes who disguise themselves to get with these two princesses whose father has hidden them at some forest retreat. One of them apparently cross-dresses as an Amazon and pulls that off well enough that the princess he's after falls in love with him, thinking the whole time that she's falling for an Amazon.

"And she goes through this crisis, right?" Millie explains, pointing her hand toward me. "Like she knows she shouldn't love a girl, but she just... accepts it. She makes this resolution to be there for her Amazon and do what she does and stuff, knowing they can't get married or have kids or anything. I mean, obviously the story doesn't end with that, but it always gets me. Like, maybe love is still as simple as that, you know? You just love someone because you do, and you just deal with that. That's majorly corny, I know," she admits after a second's silence, leaning forward with a chuckle. "But I'm a pretty shameless romantic."

I admit that I'm a romantic too, with a goofy smile.

There's nothing else I can really say now. Having to work with Millie and know her situation is bad enough, but having her here in my cabin, admitting her shyness and showing off her clearly active mind?

Before, I worried I'd get myself in trouble by losing control and making out with her or something. Now I realize that something much worse could happen if I let it.

Assuming she doesn't have some secretly repulsive habit, like maybe smoking or something, Millie is the kind of girl I could *love*. Probably crazily. The thought terrifies me.

As politely as I can, I ask her to leave. It's getting late, and I want to sleep because I wake up at five thirty no matter what. She jokingly apologizes for being a boring book nerd but leaves anyway.

"Sleep well," she says, smiling tiredly as she heads out the door.

Obviously, I do not sleep. My brain is filled with a maze of never-ending, circular thoughts that go nowhere and mean nothing. Oh, and guilt. Lots of guilt.

Sometime later, there is another knock at the door. One single knock this time. Polite and inoffensive.

"Hey, Andrea," I call.

My girlfriend immediately comes in and sits beside me, rubbing my back. She smells strongly of campfire smoke. "How are you doing now?"

"Better," I lie.

She snuggles herself under my covers and kisses my neck.

"I missed you this evening," I say, deciding not to list the reasons why it's true.

"That's sweet," Andrea replies in a low voice, slowly wrapping her legs, then her arms, around me and pressing herself close. "You're always thinking of me, huh?"

She's sort of right. Up until recently, she's taken up more than her share of my headspace. Even when she isn't pressed into me and kissing me gently on the neck before moving on to my ear, which makes her kind of hard to ignore, I'm usually thinking about her.

But now, she shares that space with a few roommates— the massive block of guilt in my head being most prominent.

Still, at times like this, she's basically everything. It's as if all parts of me just unite in their desire to be as close as possible to this little geek, who I, thanks to a brief flash of courage, call my girlfriend. Like some kind of deep instinct is telling me that anything but a full-on merging of our two selves just won't be enough.

Times like this, I can even forget that striking girl with the sad story and the active mind.

Unfortunately, it can't last—not here. My thoughts are drowned in Andrea only for a moment before worry resurfaces. We are too visible. We could potentially be seen by anyone, including Millie, who possibly still doesn't know I have a girlfriend and maybe thinks she has a chance with me.

A chance that I'm not yet willing to give up, if I'm honest with myself.

All the air in my lungs escapes, leaving me breathless, as I sigh in exasperation.

With a much shallower kind of instinct, I roll away from my girlfriend. She'll take offense, obviously, but there isn't anything I can do.

I want to, but I just can't.

Chapter Six

I get used to eating breakfast alone after that first day.

Bailey's only good for one six o'clock breakfast run per summer. She's the same way with early mornings as she is with hugs. She starts strong but realizes at some point that she actually hates getting up early and backs off. And everyone else at Lunaside is basically the same.

Well, except Jude. She's an early riser like me, but she spends that time doing these psychotic sprint workouts down on the beach. It's the only time of day where she won't catch stares for being the crazy girl blasting along the shore at ten-plus miles an hour.

But eating alone isn't so bad. Now that we're at the end of the first week, I've gotten pretty settled into a comfy little routine of shooting out of bed at five-thirty, hanging out on my step until the cafeteria opens, and then heading there for my daily dose of food-based solitude.

That ritual is shattered on Friday, though. I'm just lounging on my step, soaking up the dawn haze that drifts over Lunaside, when I notice a jovial-looking old woman in a white pantsuit and sunglasses ominously emerging from the mist.

"Madeline?" I ask. She's smiling, as if she knows she is interrupting my much-needed alone time and is reveling in it.

The camp owner takes off her sunglasses and waves. "Moira!"

I wave back in spite of myself. As relaxed as she is, Madeline Jarre isn't the kind of woman who can be snubbed.

"Beautiful morning, isn't it?" she shouts as she walks toward my perch on the doorstep.

In a bewildered monotone, I tell her it is.

She looks at me and then laughs good-naturedly. "Moira, my dear, I know I'm an intimidating old dragon, but feel free to breathe any time."

I hadn't even noticed I was holding my breath, but evidently I am. I quietly exhale.

"Better?" she asks, staring at me with her steel-gray eyes. "Anyway, I'm just here on a bit of business. I was told you get up early, so I thought I'd catch you before camp started."

Business? What business idea can possibly involve me? My best guess is that she wants me to paint a mural for Lunaside, although I can't see how that will make money for the camp.

"You see, Jeremy and I have been tossing around ideas for what we should be doing with this Film Camp. My plan was to have the camp produce something we could put up on our website when Luna gets around to programming that for us. My initial idea was to do a documentary."

Jeremy, evidently not his polite self when it comes to film stuff, shot that down right away. He straight-up told her that a documentary would seem stuffy and out-of-date to today's kids and would waste every camp's time. Instead, he proposed doing short webisodes about Lunaside's highlights.

"Do you know what a webisode is, Moira?" Madeline asks, raising her eyebrow. "Because I didn't."

I tell her I don't.

She informs me that Jeremy's idea is to do a bunch of short five-to-ten minute episodes about Lunaside and then post them on the website. He insisted that the episodes needed a main character—one of the counselors, naturally—to tie them together. His working title is *The Lunaside Girl*, named for the counselor who'll act as the "face" of Lunaside. The plan is to have her show off the camp's strengths by experiencing them directly in a fun, accessible way.

She thrusts her hands into her pockets. "So I suggested you. I thought you and Ewan made a good team on *Tastes of Trundle Island*, and this will justify your salary a bit more. With only five campers, a few dropouts could possibly have cost you your job. No pressure or anything, though. I want this web series to have a relaxed feel to it, just like the usual atmosphere around here."

I want to ask her why, if she wants a relaxed feel, she cast me, but instead I just mutter a quick, "Well, I'll do my best."

Madeline smiles at my response and thanks me for my time. Then she jokes about how almost-old ladies need their morning coffee more than anyone and heads back into the now-dissipating morning haze, leaving me to consider exactly what it is I just agreed to do.

***

I don't see Jeremy until he leaves his cabin and heads to the cafeteria at about a half hour before drop-off time. Evidently his co-counselor is not awake yet.

I grab another tea, so he won't be eating alone, and decide to hear out his idea. Telling him how putting me in front of a camera is a colossal mistake that will probably get all of us fired wouldn't be that helpful anyway. Besides, he'll figure it out for himself soon enough.

But once I start listening to him and realize how passionate he is about directing these webisodes for Lunaside, I have to admit I start to feel a bit enthusiastic. It'll still be a disaster, but he at least makes me feel like it'll be a *fun* disaster.

"I really want to capture that sort of loose, quirky humor that you see a lot these days, but give it an anchor in

Lunaside," he explains. "And honestly, I think I'm satisfied with Madeline's choice. I know we don't know each other that well, but you've got the right look for the part."

"Right look?" I ask, just like I had when Millie did that stupid pretend-director pose. Every indie kid's dream girl, indeed.

Jeremy is more matter-of-fact about it than Millie was. "Well, you're tall, thin, and pretty, which sets you up for most roles. But you've also got freckles and red hair, which I think gives you a very 'summer camp' vibe. It'll be fun seeing you going around having adventures at all the other camps. Plus, you've got serious ties to this camp. And you grew up down the road. You've basically got Lunaside running through your veins."

I start to think of a comeback about how his last point makes no sense, but Andrea just then comes through the cafeteria's double doors. Without worrying about breakfast, she hops over to us and asks what we're doing.

Jeremy explains the situation, and she sits down across from me, smiling. "Jeremy's right. And also, you've said it yourself: Lunaside changed your life last summer. It means more to you than probably anyone else. And now you get to work on a project with your girlfriend! How could you not be in love with this place?"

I open my mouth to protest but can't. First of all, she's right. I love Lunaside very deeply, no arguing that. But what really glues whatever words I might have said to my tongue is the fact that her openness has once again drawn an audience—this time in the form of poor Jeremy, who just wanted to geek out about his film project. At least she hasn't kissed me in front of him.

But then she leans forward and does that too. Just a light tap on my lips, but still. I look to Jeremy for some kind of shocked reaction that'd justify me huffing away from the table, but he isn't even looking at us. Almost like he's seen enough girls kissing that he understands proper protocol for when it happens.

Andrea grins. "Welcome aboard, Lunaside Girl."

***

On Monday, Jeremy, Andrea, and their camp show up at Art Camp's circle. I'd put them off from filming on Friday with an official-sounding lie about how we were studying impressionism, but now Jeremy is insisting that he really can't afford to waste more time. If they are going to have any time left at all in the six weeks of camp for editing, filming needs to happen now.

Seeing the logic in that, I swallow my anxiety and ask them how they want the first webisode to go.

Turns out, their plan is pretty painless. They want me to introduce myself, talk about how I live down the road and am into art, and then do an unscripted activity with my campers. Seeing as I just wing Art Camp eighty percent of the time, unscripted is easy.

I gather my campers into a circle and tell them to do another drawing based on their interests.

Luckily, Jeremy hasn't yet picked up his camera when Shapiro yells, "Oh, that is so stupid! At least steal an idea from one of us!"

"I'm sorry," I answer, taking a deep, calming breath. "But most artists really value any time they can get for personal projects."

She wrinkles her nose. "Huh. Well, I guess I could just try to draw you again or something."

As she stares at her closed drawing book, with a frown somewhere between pensive and petulant, Allie lightly taps her on the shoulder and says, "Shapiro, if you've got drawer's block, maybe you could sit with me and help me with my comic? I'm giving my main character a little sister. I don't have a real sister, so I thought it'd make the comic strip seem less like it's totally about me."

Shapiro folds her arms. "Little sister? No offense, but I think we're the same age."

"I'm almost fourteen," Allie giggles. Since she's a pretty tiny person who makes herself look even smaller with her shy, shrunken posture, she's probably used to people underestimating her age. "How old are you?"

"Eleven," she grumbles.

Allie clears her throat. "Anyway, um, I was thinking that the little sister could be, you know, smarter and prettier than my character and just frustratingly good at things. I think it'll make for some good jokes. But I think I'd need a model, you know? Otherwise, I'll just draw myself again, and that's kind of silly."

"Yeah, that'd be dumb. You can use me if you want," Shapiro replies, crawling across the grass to where Allie is sitting.

"Great!" squeals the girl who has probably just rescued the Art Camp webisode from disaster.

Once everyone has either found a project or paired up with someone who has, I let Jeremy set up his camera while the film campers sit themselves down in the grass behind him, armed with notepads.

"Let's go, Lunaside Girl," Andrea says, flashing a thumbs-up once Jeremy has started filming.

Unscripted ends up being harder than I'd imagined. As soon as Jeremy points the camera at me, I freeze. I do my best not to make that totally obvious by quickly following up with my introduction, rambling on only a little too much about Trundle Island, but I am basically motionless the whole time. Still, neither of my directors tell me they want to restart. Maybe they've already decided to make that scene a voiceover.

When Andrea tells me to talk to the campers, I'm more

confident. I immediately squat on the ground next to Emma.
Not that the other campers have dull interests, but she is Bug
Girl. That's the kind of thing practically made for webisodes.
Also, of all the campers, she's sitting the farthest away from
Shapiro, which hopefully reduces my chances of being
snarked at on camera.

"So, Emma," I start, looking at my camper's drawing
book. She's drawn some kind of insect head with humongous
eyes. "What're you drawing today?"

She keeps her eyes fixed on her drawing book. "A
Japanese Giant Hornet."

"Oh," I reply, not having heard of such a thing and not
being entirely sure I want to.

But Emma goes on, "They're really amazing little
creatures. Did you know that only a few of them can destroy
a full hive of European bees? I guess I feel bad for the bees,
but it's fascinating."

"It is. Thanks for sharing."

I quickly move on to Terrence. Superheroes probably
aren't as quirky as bugs, but maybe they're a little less
violent.

Terrence, who does look up from his drawing book,
proudly lets me know that his latest superhero creation is
Bug Girl. He explains that she has a variety of insect powers,
like the strength of an ant and the speed of a cockroach. With
a grin, he holds up his half-finished drawing. It already has
ornate moth wings, wide white pools where the character's
eyes should be, and seemingly randomly placed bug legs
sticking out from the drawing's arms, legs, shoulders, and
feet.

"That's very creative, Terrence!" I say, resolving to help
him make his designs a little less busy at some point.

He tells the camera that he hopes he can use Bug Girl
in the comic he's planning for the end of Art Camp, which
makes me smile. It makes my campers look like the kind of

kids who have goals, possibly because they have such an in-charge and talented counselor.

I then move on to Neil, hoping for an even better response because he's already a somewhat talented artist for his age. But all I get is him shyly whispering into my ear that he'd rather not appear on camera.

Respecting that, I start into an improvised speech that wraps up the episode, summarizing what Art Camp is about and inviting viewers to tune in next time.

Andrea raises one finger in the air, shutting me down. "Hey, why don't you interview those other two girls? We have time for that. Your camp's small, so I think it'd be nice to give some screen time to every camper who wants it."

I try to protest that Allie is shy and won't want to do it, but Allie herself quickly protests that she's not that shy when she's talking about her comic strip work. So we end up doing a scene where she talks about how there are lots of types of comic strips, and how she thinks it's really brilliant the way some comic strip authors can set up a joke in one page or less. It's all impressive; she clearly knows her stuff, and the strip she shows the camera looks competent enough. It's what will inevitably come after her talk that makes me not want to include her.

Sure enough, when Allie has finished gushing about all the different ways to draw a comic strip, Shapiro introduces herself and then blurts, "Moira's the laziest counselor I have ever met."

I look at my directors, imploring them to cut the filming.

When they don't, she follows up with, "But it's just because she's so talented. Like, she doesn't have to work like normal people do. Art Camp's the best camp I've ever gone to, and my dad's been putting me in summer camps since I was a baby. And a lot of them have been specialty camps. I've done hiking and ballet, and I even got put in a reading camp that the library back home put on, but this one's my favorite. I begged my dad to let me go again this year."

She flashes a surprisingly cute smile that makes her look her actual age for once, then looks at Allie. "Hey! Maybe your pretend little sister could be in Art Camp?"

"Uh, maybe," replies Allie, sounding as bewildered as I feel.

Andrea, with a smile that suggests she is holding back a laugh, motions for me to wrap the scene. I give my concluding spiel, without interruption this time. Andrea gives me another thumbs-up, and that's it.

When Jeremy has packed up his camera, he walks over to me and shakes my hand. "Great work! I know we put you on the spot, but I think you pulled through. Don't get too hung up about things flowing perfectly. Like I said, I want these little episodes to have a loose, unscripted feel to them."

I nod. "O-okay."

"And I have to say, kudos to your campers! Getting kids in front of a camera is often a disaster waiting to happen, but I think your guys made the most of it."

"Well, um, thanks."

"Hey, no problem. I'm just happy to be moving forward with this project," he says.

Once he starts arranging his campers into a double-file line, Andrea comes over to where I'm standing and takes my hands. "You were wonderful."

I immediately pull away. For one thing, one episode's worth of fumbling probably doesn't deserve that much praise. And, well, there's also the fact that some of her campers are looking at us. Mine have already gone back to drawing, but who knows what would happen if Shapiro caught a glance of us like this?

"Thanks," I mumble, "I was sure I'd mess up."

Her momentary sad frown tells me that I hadn't messed up until just then. "You've got an easy grace in front of the camera. I really enjoy watching you do your thing," she says breathlessly, gazing up into my eyes.

I look away. "I'm sure you do. But don't you have a camp to run? We can chat later about this."

She mutters that I'm probably right. Then she runs off to join Jeremy at the head of Film Camp's impressively organized line as the group heads to the cafeteria, not bothering to look back at me for even a second.

Chapter Seven

That same day, just after Shapiro—the last of my campers to leave, as usual—leaves with her dad, Jeremy finds me sitting on the grass and taps me on the shoulder.

I jump.

He waves meekly. "Hey, sorry to scare you."

I assure him he didn't scare me, even though he did.

"Uh, I don't want to overwork you, but I was kinda hoping that we could shoot our initial episode this evening."

"Didn't you already do that? Wasn't that Art Camp?" I ask, staring dubiously at the camera that's sitting on the grass beside my director.

"Yeah, I thought it was, but apparently Madeline had an idea this afternoon. Now, she wants to do kind of an intro episode thing, like a montage with a voiceover or something. I figured we could splice in footage from the other episodes, but she suggested a more detailed voiceover, where you talk about Luna and the counselors, as well as yourself and Trundle Island."

"And you want me to do that now?"

"I was hoping?" he answers, following it up with his kind, baby-faced smile, so as to make saying no impossible. This boy is a born director, all right.

"Argh, fine. But after this, one filming session per day, okay?"

He winks. "You got it."

So, without further protest from me, he and I work through quite a few takes that involve me introducing Lunaside and then stopping midsentence or forgetting to mention that Luna, who's actually a well-known professor of education, has "doctor" in front of her name. Throughout it all, Jeremy keeps me calm with his never-ending supply of patience and reassuring smiles that suggest I'm not that bad of an actor, in spite of all the awkwardness. It soon becomes one of those rare, shining moments in my life where I'm filled with the pride that comes from being almost decent at something.

That moment lasts only until the other counselors start to gather around us. Absorbed as he is in filming, Jeremy doesn't seem to notice them at all even though the sight of them makes me choke on my own voice. But, not wanting to let my helpful director down, I do my best. Eventually, he shuts off his camera and tells me, "That's great. I can work with this for now. Thanks for being patient."

But the Lunasiders do not leave. They have questions; they have comments.

Jude slaps my shoulder and laughs. "Mo, you are such a boss sometimes. You just made that up on the spot? That is talent right there."

"Jeremy helped me," I reply, folding my arms sheepishly at her frank compliment.

She frowns at my director, then shakes his hand and adds, "Ah, I guess you deserve a bit of credit too. Good work, man."

"Uh, thanks," he replies, suddenly becoming fixated on adjusting his glasses.

Then Bailey comes over to us and proposes a wardrobe upgrade for the Lunaside Girl. But Rory chases her off by taking her suggestion as an excuse to start up a conversation with her about her own fashion choices.

Even Layla compliments us. She gives me a light tap on

the back and shoots me an encouraging wink. "If I'd half of your intuitive grace on the stage, I probably wouldn't be stuck playing kid roles all the time."

Jeremy points out that she'd also have to stop looking like a kid to do that, but she ignores him and goes back to standing beside Millie, who's been entirely silent this whole time. Eventually, Andrea comes up to us, looking a bit confused. "So you guys filmed the intro?"

"Yeah, it was just a quick run-through," explains Jeremy. "You were eating, so I didn't want to interrupt."

"Oh," she replies, with a half-frown that suggests she would have preferred the interruption. "Well, from what I saw, you were great."

"Thanks. I always appreciate your unbiased opinion," I joke.

Jeremy taps his stomach dramatically, looking at Andrea and me. "Okay, now I'm wishing that I hadn't interrupted my own supper for that, because I'm starving. If you'd like to join me, I could give you a better sense of Madeline's ever-changing game plan. That way, you won't get left out of the loop next time?"

"Okay, that works! Do you want to come too, Moira?" she chirps.

While I would like spending some time with my girlfriend after such a long day, she'll be mostly there with Jeremy. And then I'll get uncomfortable every time she does something to remind him that we're a couple. Not only that, but today's double dose of filming has annihilated whatever energy I had. It's possible that I'll pass out long before I get a chance to be embarrassed.

I decide there's no point in lying. "Uh, actually I think I'm going to head home for the night. All of that filming left me worn out, and I sort of just want to crawl into my own bed and cocoon myself until I recover."

She smiles and gives me a light kiss. "Aw, my little

introvert. Well, you get your rest, and I'll see you in the morning?"

"Very *late* morning," I tease, moving away from her just enough that she won't take that comment as an excuse to kiss me again in front of everyone.

"Funny. Anyway, I'll text you good night later. I'd call, but I know you like to sleep at early o'clock, so I won't."

"'Early o'clock.' Really?"

"What? I'm not a super-talented actor who can just ad-lib all day like you," she says.

"Doofus," I reply. "See you tomorrow! Oh, and thanks for making me not feel like a terrible actor, Jeremy."

"Any time," he chuckles, giving me a nerdy little salute as the two of them head toward the cafeteria.

I start for home not long after that, making sure to let Bailey—who is conveniently sitting on her bed reading a magazine when I find her—know she'll be having the cabin to herself for the night.

"Everything okay?" she asks, raising an eyebrow.

"Sure," I answer.

That doesn't sound too convincing in my head, so I continue with, "Yeah, everything's fine. I'm just drained from all the filming today."

"Huh. Well, have fun," she sings.

As I hit the path, the sky is just starting to turn orange, making the ragged-looking clouds appear purple and pink and orange and maybe blue all at once. There's no breeze, really, but the air is just cool enough that it isn't necessary. With a grin, I take off my sandals and start walking the well-worn, sandy, white path barefoot. Being alone with the scenery like this is rejuvenating, almost like I've already forgotten my post-filming exhaustion.

Except, as it turns out, I'm not alone.

"Hey there," Millie greets me, as if she's just been walking this path and happened to run into me. "Good job on the filming today. You're very talented."

"Uh, thanks," I answer, letting her fall into step with me.

"I didn't tell you earlier because—Well, you know why probably."

I look down and see that Millie is barefoot too, and is carrying her black flip-flops in her hand. "Shy, right?"

"Heh, yeah. So where're you headed? I love walking this path, but I'm a Trundle Island rookie. I'm scared to leave it in case I run into a bear or something."

I laugh. "There aren't any bears on the island."

"Oh. Well, maybe a wolf, then?"

"Maybe a wolf. Anyway, I'm heading home. Filming really drained me, and I just want to recharge in my own space. You said you were shy, so you must know what I'm talking about."

"Well, yeah, obviously," she mumbles.

Walking with Millie is different than walking with Andrea, who is usually the only person I walk with otherwise. At times like this, Andrea says something once in a while to let me know that she appreciates my scenery drunkenness. With Millie there's silence, as if she gets scenery drunk too.

When we get to my house, I almost hate to go inside and leave her there. Scenery drunk or not, she seems like maybe she doesn't like solitude as much as I do.

"Hey, do you want some tea or something?" I offer.

She gives a surprised laugh, as if she's one of those people who thinks it's just for old ladies and hipsters. "Tea?"

"Yes, tea! I guess you didn't know it's the official drink of Trundle Island, huh?"

"Apparently not," she admits, following me toward the house.

So we have tea. For myself, I make a cup of organic loose-leaf jasmine green. I stuff the leaves into a tea ball, instead of getting out my handmade ceramic pot, because I don't know Millie well enough to show off just how much of a tea geek I am. Then I throw a bag of some by-now-ancient chamomile blend into a cup for Millie. A tea so bland that she can't possibly hate it.

When I get to the table and start dipping my tea ball into the hot water, Millie eyes it with a smiling frown. "You're pretty hardcore with this tea stuff, huh?"

I anxiously drop the ball into the cup, splashing boiling water onto my hand. Ouch. "Uh, well, I just know what I like, I guess?"

She takes a sip of her own tea and nods. "Heh, it's cool. It's like me and books."

After a moment's silence, she adds, "Do you read much?"

Seeing the eager gleam in her white eyes makes me quietly admit that I don't read as much as I probably should, although I do read lots of books about artistic technique, vegan cooking, and tea. It's not a lie, and makes me sound at least somewhat smart. Hopefully.

But Millie just presses her thin lips together in a way that suggests she's amused, rather than impressed, by my reading material.

"Tea is a surprisingly intellectual topic," I explain. "It's got a lot of history, and there's a lot of art inspired by tea."

Millie then smiles warmly, baring two rows of strangely small, perfectly white teeth. They don't match her world-weary face. These are inexperienced-looking teeth, teeth that haven't seen much in the way of caffeine or dental disasters or anything. It also means that she likely doesn't smoke, which complicates life for me. If she were a smoker, I could just let her go right now.

"Do you read any, like, novels, though?" she asks in a tone that sounds more curious than disappointed. Like it's not enough that I read—she wants us to have common ground for some reason.

I laugh. Novels? I read lots of those early nineteen

hundreds children's novels when I was a kid, because I loved the long-winded descriptions of scenery. My favorite was *Anne of Green Gables*, which was lucky. Being a tall redhead who lives on a small island means that, eventually, every family relative will gift you a copy, thinking how clever they are for making the connection.

But recently? Only two, and those are hidden beneath my mattress still, four years later.

"Uh, a couple," I admit.

Apparently sensing my discomfort, she leans forward and raises an eyebrow. "Guilty pleasures, huh? Come on, you can tell me the titles. There are no trashy books, only trashy readers."

I tell her the titles, even though I don't want to. Counting only two obscure lesbian young adult novels that I found online during a burst of once-in-a-lifetime courage and computer skills among the only novels I've read in four years makes me seem a lot more politically gay, and also more illiterate, than I am.

Millie's whitish eyes flicker gleefully. "I can't say I've heard of them, but hey, do you think I could look at them?"

For some reason, I tell her she can. I tell her to wait at the table while I get them because she'll probably think it's a bit childish that I still keep books beneath my mattress.

She laughs at the first cover of the first book, *Seduction*. It's a photo of two dark-haired girls who look like supermodels, awash in eerie purplish-blue light. One of the girls is standing; she is pouting, while draping her arms seductively around the other girl, who is seated. They are both wearing black cocktail dresses.

"Wow," Millie breathes between laughs. "Just... And how long have you had this?"

"Four years, give or take," I reply, sliding the other book into her view.

She grabs the other one and stares at it. The cover isn't as outrageous. It's made to look like lined paper, and has a dull, standard font that says *I Love You, Anna K.*

"That one was really sappy," I explain, hoping to move on from that first book. "But I liked it. It's about a girl who falls in love with her next-door neighbor, and throughout the whole novel she's writing this all-encompassing love poem that she's going to give her to admit her love. Then one night they're at this dinner party with their families, and they're sitting on the porch and she just says it. Anna says it back. They kiss. The main character makes some point about how that moment, the living of it, was the real poetry. The end."

Millie sighs. "Heh, if only, eh?"

"You mean the poem thing?" I ask, meeting her gaze. "Because I did that."

She shakes her head. "I didn't mean the poem—Hold on, you did what?"

I smile nonchalantly. "The first girl I loved. I did that. I wrote her a poem and gave it to her."

"Whoa," she responds, her ghost eyes wide. "Gutsy."

I shrug, enjoying the feeling of being considered more experienced in love matters than this girl who is at least a year older than me. And it isn't a lie. I'd been in love with Jude as long as I knew I liked girls, and, when we were fourteen, I gave her a love poem to confess that. She liked the poem but made it very clear that she didn't like girls.

Of course I leave out the part where I cried for days after Jude rejected me, and I neglect to mention that this girl is also my best friend and, now, coworker at Lunaside. But it's still a nice feeling.

With a self-deprecating laugh, Millie just shakes her head. "I could never. I'm too white bread. I grew up in this perfect little picket-fence suburban world. You know, the kind of place where strong feelings are kind of smiled and 'uh-uh'd out of you at a young age."

I spend a bit of time figuring out how to respond to that

without encouraging Millie to write me a love poem. But as I ponder, Mom casually wanders into the room, and I derail that train of thought just in time to grab my books and sit on them. Well, I sit on *Seduction*. Being the safer of the two, I put *I Love You, Anna K.* in my lap.

Mom quietly goes over to the counter and makes herself a cup of tea as well. And then she sits with us, like that's something she always does. She at least isn't wearing her work clothes now. In her oversized forest-green V-neck sweater, she actually looks like a real mom and not just a therapist who moonlights as an awkward maternal figure.

When she sits down in the chair between Millie and me, she immediately gives me an apologetic smile. "I'm sorry, Moira. I didn't want to interrupt your time with your, hmm, friend, but I was sitting in the living room and I couldn't help but overhear you two talking—"

"About books," I say, smiling.

Of course. Mom isn't here to lecture me on how I shouldn't be so girl-crazy. She's here because, underneath it all, she's an unrepentant book nerd who is responding to a call no one with proper social skills would answer.

I hold out a hand, pointing my palm at Millie, and then do the same for Mom. "Mom, this is Millie. Millie, this is my mom, Philoméne."

"Call me Phil," Mom protests with a surprisingly congenial smile.

"Will do," answers Millie with a nod.

The two of them then start chatting about books—famous books they hate that everyone else loves, books that they think speak to their lives, stuff like that—leaving me feeling like maybe I should have introduced them as soon as we got into the house. That would have saved me from showing off my pathetic duo of novels.

While those two are off in their own world, I go and make myself another cup of tea. I repeat that a few more times until finally there's a break in the conversation because Mom asks a question that Millie just can't answer. She frowns and leans her elbows onto the table and sucks the last vestiges of her weak chamomile tea out of her cup. But she can't answer the question.

Mom had put her hands in front of her, like she always does when she's excited, and had asked, "Okay, here's a question: Who is your all-time favorite author?"

And so here Millie is, furrowing her brow with such gravity that it's as if Mom has asked her to reverse entropy. Mom had already admitted that she didn't have a favorite. She confided that it was a theoretically infinite tie between Virginia Woolf, Sylvia Plath, Emily Dickinson, Christina Rossetti, and other such troubled, reclusive women.

Millie is not placated by Mom's multifarious cop-out answer. Evidently, she's the kind of girl who gives important answers to important questions.

But then, suddenly, she laughs and says, "Sorry, I think there are too many. I don't think I have a favorite author."

Mom smiles at her and shakes her head, but that's the end of it.

Their book conversation basically dries up at that second. It isn't long before my mother admits that all this chatting about books has made her eager to read a bit before bed, and she's gone. Then I put our teacups away, wash them out, and that's it.

Millie puts on her flip-flops and heads onto our porch. Since she hasn't said good-bye, I assume I am to follow her. When I get outside, she's sitting on the edge of our porch, staring into the distance.

"Sir Philip Sidney," she blurts.

"Huh? Who?" I ask, sitting beside her.

She keeps staring ahead. "The guy who wrote *The Arcadia*. He's my favorite author. He died young, you know. Not a lot of his stuff made it to us. I felt kinda shy admitting that to your mom, I guess."

I keep quiet. Somehow, I feel that my instinct to say "that's too bad" would seem silly and immature.

"We just read bits of that book for a class, but I went and looked him up 'cause I'm a nerd like that. And I just got struck with this bright guy who never seemed to be able to get his start in life, even though everyone liked him, and then he just died in some random battle, with all these great works left half-written."

After I continue to say nothing, she starts to get up but doesn't stop talking. "Then there was this girl. She inspired the only major piece he ever finished."

She starts walking away, but slowly.

I know I am probably walking into something dangerous, but I haven't said anything in a while so I ask, "Okay, I give. Why was she so important?"

She just smiles her sleepy smile and says, "He loved her. He couldn't have her, and he had to figure out how to deal with that. Guess his solution was to write. 'Night, Moira."

"Good night, Millie," I reply, letting her brave the nonexistent bears and possible wolves on the path back to Lunaside alone.

Chapter Eight

Our next webisode is about Sports Camp. We shoot it the Wednesday of that same week. It turns out a little differently because Jude is leading instead of me. Filming starts around ten o'clock, and she makes all of us regret that by the time the quite hot sun is almost ready to hit its noonish peak.

For some reason, she thought it'd be a good idea to get all of us—Sports Camp, Art Camp, and Film Camp, along with Rory, Andrea, and me—to be part of her workout. Only Jeremy is spared, because he's working the camera. The rest of us are stuck doing jumping jacks, push-ups, sit-ups, and whatever else she feels like barking at us until we faint from heat exhaustion.

My campers seem to be handling it all surprisingly well. Allie and Shapiro dutifully keep up with every one of her commands, their eyes fixed on her the entire time like soldiers running drills. Terrence and Neil lag behind and have poor form, and Emma sort of hides behind the film campers and fakes it, but I'm impressed with them all. None of them are dying like I am.

"Jude!" I yell, while being forced to do another round of jumping jacks. "Wouldn't it be better if you spoke about yourself and your camp? I'm sure the parents would love hearing that the head of Sports Camp is—" I want to finish with "a national-class rugby star," but my lungs tell me I've used up my air quota already.

Jude laughs. "Sorry, Mo, I'm pretty sure my workouts speak for themselves. Plus, your guys are doing well. You should be proud."

Yes, my "guys" are doing well. But me? Can't she see that I am drowning in a pool of my own sweat?

But she probably does notice. She tosses me a bottle of water and says, "You're not doing so bad yourself, Lunaside Girl."

I catch the bottle and chug about half of it immediately. "Uh, thanks."

She then hands water to my campers and Film Camp. "See, that wasn't so bad, huh? I'm a bit hardcore, but I know what's enough."

My brother, who's apparently only fared a little better than I have, takes a huge gulp of water and pants, "Keep telling yourself that, you maniac."

Jude looks at him and smiles. "But I don't accept backtalk. Ten laps, Connell."

He gestures to everyone who isn't in Sports Camp. "Aw, come on. Not in front of everyone!"

"Yes, in front of everyone. I wouldn't want viewers to think I'm soft. Especially not on my assistant!" She laughs.

"Argh, fine. But if I come back with heatstroke, it's on your head."

She smiles smugly. "Okay, but when you finish and you're not dead or in a coma, I suggest you look up the definition of heatstroke, champ."

He grumbles and starts running.

When he leaves, Jeremy turns off his camera. Seeing the opening, Jude then walks over and starts teasing him about how she'll get him training next time. All the campers seemingly take that as unspoken permission to have social time and split off into their various little cliques, with Art Camp huddling together and chatting amongst themselves. Shapiro, of course, sits outside their circle and stares at nothing.

Amidst the crowd, Andrea finds me. She claps her hands to her knees. "Great workout, huh?" Her face is glistening, but she doesn't look tired—no doubt because, unlike me, Andrea actually works out. She's no Jude, but she and her mother take classes at the gym near their house and lift weights together. Basically just stuff that I can't picture my mom and I doing together in a million years. Or even separately. We Connells, other than Rory, I guess, are not known for our athletic ambition.

"I'm dead," I confess. "I am literally going to melt."

She chuckles and takes a drink from her own bottle of water. "Aw, well, you sure looked good failing at all those exercises. I *knew* you'd look irresistible in the uniform," she adds with an approving glance at my backside.

"Creep," I joke. "But you look okay in it too."

Because I knew Jude would do this to us, I warned Andrea and we'd both worn the uniform. She'd chosen the light blue version of our camp t-shirt—it came in basically every color imaginable, because Luna wants everyone to feel comfortable—along with shiny sapphire-colored soccer shorts. She also has on running shoes for once. They're white, and show off just how adorably tiny her feet are.

She waves away my compliment. "I'm all right, I guess. But I'm just a little snub compared to you, my beautiful, uncoordinated failure of an athlete."

I'm going to ask her what a snub is, and maybe tease her about that mouthful of a compliment, but then I notice that everyone, including Andrea, has suddenly turned toward the cafeteria. Wrapped up in preparing my comeback as I was, I missed why they'd done that. But then I look too, and it all makes sense.

Drama Camp is slowly heading toward us. They're walking in formation, with Layla and Millie in front and the campers arranged in two lines of ten. Even Bailey is there, walking alongside everyone, looking quite a bit like a younger, thinner, taller Madeline in her loose black pantsuit.

But it isn't that they've just suddenly appeared. At least, it isn't for me. It's what Layla and Millie—but maybe just Millie, if I'm being honest—are wearing.

Bailey has apparently been very busy. Because here are the Drama Camp counselors, now standing on the sidelines of the Lunaside field with their campers, in green-and-white cheerleading outfits.

Their tops are just white, shorter-sleeved versions of the Lunaside t-shirt, with the logo in a nondescript shade of green that flatters both Layla's light brown complexion and Millie's paleness. But Bailey has also given them these white, frilled, knee-length skirts trimmed with that same green. Apparently they convinced Millie to ditch the flip-flops because they're both also wearing white running shoes. Oh, and they're holding matching pom-poms.

Seriously.

We all stare in awe as Layla and Millie start up a cheer routine while they stifle smiles that suggest they think this is the most hilarious thing in the world.

"Sports Camp's the best!" they yell.

"Forget about the rest!" yell their campers back.

"Except maybe Drama!" everyone cheers in unison, causing laughter to erupt from their accidental audience.

Jude, whose deep roar of a laugh rises above everyone else's, tells Jeremy that he should grab his camera. Evidently he agrees, and starts filming again.

Without another word, they break into this really elaborate dance routine. Campers standing on each other and pulling moves that look kind of like hip-hop dancing. Layla shouts things, directing the campers into their positions. Millie just stands still, cheering quietly. She seems to be having fun but is clearly too shy to really get into it.

I can't help but smile in spite of myself. No question, she

looks mind-blowing in that outfit, as dumb and cliché as it is. It makes me hate Bailey and her sewing skills a little for making me feel things I don't want to feel. But it isn't just that. Seeing her there, shyly doing her best to follow along with Layla even though she isn't outgoing enough to pull it off, just gives me this weird feeling in my chest. Kind of like I'm staring at a much better-looking version of myself. Saying it's surreal is an understatement.

Luckily, Andrea snaps me out of it. She wraps one of her arms around my waist and says, "So, what would I have to do to get you into one of those?"

"First? Buy *a lot* of fabric," I joke, grateful for the distraction.

"That could be arranged," she whispers.

We just stand there like that until the pretend cheerleaders finish their routine. Then Jeremy, apparently not built for such a hot day, lumbers over to us and taps me on the shoulder.

"Hey," he says, wiping sweat from his forehead, "I know I promised only one per day. But, uh, this seems like too good of an opportunity to get some awesome footage."

"You just want to find a place for the girls in the cheerleader costumes in your project!" I tease, waving a finger at him. That isn't fair, and I know it. Jeremy has so far been nothing but respectful—sometimes laughably so—to all of us girls in his time at Lunaside. But I am not going near Millie, especially not with her looking like that.

"Um," he says, biting his lip and lowering his head in a way that makes me feel like I'm the only one who wants the girls in the cheerleader costumes in the project, even though he's the one filming everything.

But we get them on camera anyway. First, I chat with Layla. She goes on about how she wasn't pretty or brave enough to do cheerleading in high school, but the combination of theatrics and athletics made her want to try it.

With a wink at me, she admits, "Then I had a lightbulb moment and wondered if we could integrate it into Drama Camp. Well, really what I thought was, 'I'm the boss here. Why not?'"

I laugh, and she goes on about cheerleading costumes for a bit before inviting Bailey to join her on camera. Bailey scowls, but she brightens a bit when I ask her how long it took her to make those skirts.

"Not long! They had a bunch of fabric ready to go! It was a bit of extra work to get those stripes on there, but the whole thing was definitely painless. I hope everyone liked the final product," she says, giving me a searching look that makes me uncomfortable. I thank her for her time and send her away immediately after that, restraining myself from literally shoving her off-camera.

Jeremy suggests that, for the sake of completeness, we also hunt down Millie. She is just then hiding in a sea of her campers, and it takes more than a few moments to get her attention. But finally we do, and she follows us to an open spot on the field.

I am not sure what my director is thinking; Millie doesn't want to be on camera. The way she stares at the ground while Jeremy explains the plan tells me she'd rather being doing anything else. Including training with Jude on the warmest day of the year. In the tropics.

"Just look at me," I find myself saying, parroting the calming words the director of *Tastes of Trundle Island* had used on me during the first few episodes.

After only a moment's hesitation, she turns her shockingly white eyes on me.

I clear my throat. "So, Millie, um, is this your first time cheerleading?"

She chuckles. "Heh, yeah."

"And how did you like it?"

She grins, showing off her perfect rows of tiny white teeth. "Fun. It was fun. I really enjoyed it."

The way she shuffles her feet as we stand there tells me that probably that's all Jeremy will get out of Millie, whether he likes it or not.

After I thank her for her time, she immediately runs back to join her camp, safe from the camera's view. Again, I have that weird feeling in my chest. Like I've just forced myself into an interview.

***

That afternoon's drawing activity is about symmetry. We lack those fancy drawing mirrors that everyone uses to draw butterflies in third grade, which is a shame. But I compensate by getting everyone to draw a line in the center of a page in their drawing books. Then I challenge them to draw something on the left that they would then match on the right.

"You could do a half drawing, like a butterfly or something. And just match it. But you could also draw a full picture on one side and then try to copy it. That's a form of symmetry."

Emma's eyes go wide. "This. Is. Going. To. Help. Me. So. Much!"

"Geez, chill out, Bug Girl," Shapiro groans, rolling her eyes as she opens her drawing book.

But Emma doesn't chill out. She doesn't even notice that Shapiro has just insulted her. She just grabs her pencil and one of the rulers I keep in my bag and starts drawing.

Hoping to keep that tongue from cutting anyone else, I look into my smallest camper's blue eyes and ask, "So, what's your symmetrical drawing going to be, Shapiro?"

She frowns at the paper. "Uh, are we allowed to do abstract art?"

"Of course! Why wouldn't you be?"

"I don't know," she says with a quick shrug. "Everyone just draws, like, regular stuff in our camp. And I know how much you hate doing real work. I just didn't want you to get mad at me for doing something complicated and making you put effort into your job."

"Draw what you want," I snap. Normally I have more patience, but it's hot and I didn't get to shower after Jude's workout because Sports Camp had to. Besides, I'm still sulky and torn about that cheerleading thing. I have no time for this precocious little brat who likes me and doesn't all at once.

I pass the afternoon answering my campers' questions about symmetry.

"Neil, drawing symmetrical waves that look realistic *is* basically impossible."

"Sure, Allie, you can just make perfectly aligned panels if you'd like."

"Yes, Terrence, it's okay if you draw a superhero whose halves don't match."

"No, Emma, I didn't know that a cockroach's wings aren't necessarily symmetrical."

Only Shapiro has nothing to ask. She frowns as she draws, her faint blonde eyebrows almost overlapping her blue eyes. Clearly there is something going on in that overactive mind of hers. Something that no doubt is half praise, half insult toward someone—probably me. But she's working, and silently. I'm happy for that, at least.

Shortly before the parents arrive, I get to see Terrence's newest creation, Half-and-Half Man, a superhero who is half-traditional superhero costume and half electricity-based creature. I compliment him on how he was able to work from the center line. I think his character's name makes him sound like a guy who is trying to be a bit healthier with his coffee, but I keep that to myself because Terrence seems to be learning from me somehow and that's what matters.

Allie shows me her drawing, too, but it's just an empty series of perfectly symmetrical panels for some future comic strip, so it's a bit less impressive.

Neil and Emma say they'll finish theirs at home. Neil has sketched some waves; they look decent, covered in eraser marks though they are. Emma has drawn exactly half a cockroach; the right side of her page is entirely blank.

"But it's a pretty nice half of a bug though, huh?" she says.

"Of course!" I shout as she heads toward her mom's car. And it really is. Emma has clearly been practicing; even her shading, which I find is usually the skill kid artists lack, is quite good. The real skill she still needs to learn is how to finish things.

When the other campers have left, Shapiro hands me her drawing book. "Uh, I was done for a while. I just didn't want those guys to see what I drew. I don't think they'd get it."

"Oh no?"

"I told you. It's kind of abstract. Just be quiet and look at it. It was just something I thought about."

I do as I am told. The first thing I see is the dark line down the center of the page. It's about as straight as could be expected—a totally respectable line. On the left of the page, she's drawn a girl. A girl wearing a sundress with a nicely detailed wave pattern. Everything beyond her forehead disappears beyond the page, and so do the tips of her toes. But it's an improvement, so I take encouragement from that.

Beyond the right side of the line, she's drawn another girl. She has shaggy hair that had been shaded and shaded and shaded until it became a very definite sort of black. None of her parts go off the page, and she's wearing a cheerleader's outfit: t-shirt, thigh-length skirt, running shoes. Her mouth is a simple straight line.

Forget about her fellow campers not getting her drawing.

I don't get it.

"Your proportions are really improving. And, okay, so that's Millie on the right. And obviously you drew me again. But why both?"

"I told you. It's abstract. It's symmetry," she replies, suddenly sounding possessed by every pretentious artist in every art gallery everywhere.

I don't ask her to explain, but she moves toward the book and does that anyway, pointing at the figures as she does so. "When I was watching Millie do the cheerleader thing, I thought she looked, you know, familiar. Then when I saw you do that interview with her, I realized that she wasn't. It was you that I was seeing. Like you guys were the same, except not. Like, she was making the same look you always make in our camp when you don't know what to do or I ask something you can't answer. Kind of closed in, like the world's about to fall on you. She looked like that. She looked like you. So it's symmetrical."

"Huh," I breathe.

"I mean, otherwise you're different. Like, Millie's way prettier. She could be a model. Your forehead is too wide for your pointy chin. It makes you look like an alien. But she's in drama, so you're the smart one. And I'll bet she can't draw like you."

As usual, I have no idea whether to feel insulted or complimented by what Shapiro says. "Thanks?"

When her dad finally arrives, I accidentally let out a really loud sigh of relief. Both the Hanleys stare at me, until I spread my arms, throw my head back, and say, "Oh, I'm just so happy that it's starting to cool off!"

"Oh yeah, today was brutal," Aidan answers, giving me a sympathetic nod.

When they leave, I treat myself to a round of collapsing onto the ground. For one thing, it's still way too hot and I still haven't showered from this morning's workout. And for another, my head had filled with thoughts and they'd all sloshed together, mixing and solidifying all day while I was melting from the heat and nervousness and guilt. Now my head is cement. Once it hits the cool grass of Lunaside, it's never coming up again.

Or so I think.

"Hey, Moira." Bailey's voice.

I don't move at all. Even if I'm not still sort of blaming her for my troubles earlier, I am not getting up for anyone. Here on the grass, I am at peace.

"I'm heading to Grandma's house for dinner. Wanna walk with me?"

Of course I don't want to walk with you, I pout in my head. *You are an evil little costume designer who put me in a difficult, and really kind of pathetic, position this morning. Cheerleaders, really? Even if I didn't have a girlfriend, I'd be mad because you made me realize I've got really tacky taste.*

But all I say in reality is, "Yeah, sure," and get up after all.

Now, Bailey's a purposeful sort of girl. I know when I agree to walk with her that it will be for a reason. She's not the strolling type and she can handle walking to her grandmother's house just fine alone. The only time I've ever seen her without a specific objective is during our late-night cabin chats, which is one of the reasons I like them so much.

Unfortunately, it is not two in the morning, and we are not in our cabin. Something is definitely up.

We make our way down the hill and onto the path that eventually leads to Madeline's house. Technically it's the same path that leads to my house, but I rarely have reason to walk past Lunaside and thus it's foreign territory. After the camp, the path begins to run parallel to hard, grayish rock cliffs instead of sandy dune slopes, so it isn't all that hard to imagine it really is a foreign country. Which is what I do to keep myself distracted from wondering why Bailey asked me to come along.

By the time she opens her mouth, I am already long gone, deep in my scenery drunkenness at the sight of the waves battering themselves uselessly against the rock cliffs. They leave this perpetual salty haze that's intoxicating. If the sun was higher, maybe it would make a rainbow.

Bailey cares not for my silly musings. "Millie's really into you."

"So?" I huff, folding my arms and de-aging by, like, ten years.

Bailey squints at the horizon, although I doubt she is charmed by the salty haze like I am. "We've become sort of close in the past few weeks—kind of like you and I did last summer. She's really smart, a total introvert, and a bit of a doofus. She's even got a nature fetish! It's almost like working with another you."

"I do not have a nature fetish," I protest, trying to ignore the fact that Bailey's voice has merged with Shapiro's in my head.

She's another you, Bailey-Shapiro insists. *It's symmetrical.*

"Listen, I'm not saying this to get a kick out of playing matchmaker. I'm saying this because you're my best friend, and Millie's moving up that chart too. And I work with her, so every day I have to listen to her go on about how pretty, awesome, and smart she thinks you are. She's falling for you, and not softly."

"You do realize I have a girlfriend, right?" I remind her, fixating on the rocky cliffs, trying to emulate their hardness so Bailey's words will just smash onto me and explode into useless spray. No rainbows.

"You know she excitedly tells me about every single time you guys meet up? She says she has fun, even though she never knows what to say because she's shy around you.

I heard she went to your house—she says Phil's a kindred spirit."

"You aren't listening," I sigh, feeling more like a sandy slope than a rocky cliff.

"She didn't want to do the cheerleader thing, you know? She said she didn't want to look so visible in front of you. Just you, like you were suddenly all of Lunaside. We eventually talked her into it because it'd be fun—"

But then suddenly I am the wave, crashing myself against my friend's endless stream of well-meaning, yet really irritating, chatter. "Bailey, come on, why'd you invite me along? What do you think this is supposed to accomplish? Do you honestly think I'm going to break up with my girlfriend to chase after some girl I barely know?"

I think we're headed for our first official fight here, but she just sighs and looks away like I'm a first grader who just cannot figure out what two and two equals. "I get that. And don't think I'm trying to break you up or something, but, like, you've been dating Andrea for what, three months?"

"Four," I correct.

"Okay, fine. You've been dating this girl for four months. It's going well for you, and I get that. But, like, call me idealistic—"

"That's the last thing I would ever call you," I growl.

"You could in this case, maybe. See, I get that you're into Andrea. She's your first girlfriend, and you haven't been together long enough for all those crazy, happy feelings to wear off. And I'm happy for you. She's cute and seems to know where's she's going in life. But, I don't know, she's not exactly the kind of person I would have imagined you with. Like, I know it sounds bad, but I kind of feel like she's not quite up to your level intellectually."

"Okay, Andrea's *not* stupid. And did you miss the part where Millie's going into her second year of university? It hardly seems fair to—"

Before I can react to that, she elbows me playfully and teases, "Chill out, Moira, I'm just making an observation. Besides, you're definitely not up to Andrea's level professionally, either. What I'm trying to say is that things are going well with her, sure. But I just think that you and Millie could be better than 'well.' For you, she could be one of those rare people that most of us never come close to meeting, you know? The kind of person you meet and then you just... know because they're sort of you and sort of not."

"Okay, fine, that *is* idealistic." Why can't Bailey see what she's doing here? She's supposed to be my best friend. Why can't she see that she's basically smashing my heart against those rocky cliffs, then holding it against the salt spray just to be a jerk?

"All I'm saying is that if you feel half as deeply for Millie as I think you do, you might be wise to give her a chance. Just get to know her better somehow. I'm not saying go out with her—just be open to the possibility. I know you're happy with Andrea, and I hope you know I'd never want to ruin that for you. But, like, do you love her?"

Silence.

Andrea and I have great chemistry. We've had that since the first time we met, since she got caught applauding during one of our on-location tapings, which happened to be in a local strawberry field. She didn't know that people don't typically applaud on-location, because she'd only ever visited studio sets. The director yelled at her. Then Dad offered her a ride to the on-set kitchen segment of the filming because he felt bad. That gave us a chance to talk. Shy as I am, I felt she was easy to talk to even then. And it's been that way ever since.

But love? That's not a word that's entered our vocabularies. Andrea is pretty loud-and-proud about being my girlfriend, but she's never claimed to love me. And I'm still having trouble admitting I have a sex drive, let alone a fully functioning heart. It just never comes up.

But then, we've never really talked about going exclusive, either. After the first date, we just *were*. I think Andrea was just excited to finally have a girlfriend, while I was so not the type to say, or even think, "No, sorry, I can't be your girlfriend. I have to go play the field."

We've never really had a serious conversation, period. It's always just light and comfortable and cozy with us. And I like that. Seriousness is painful; lightness is safe.

Eventually, Bailey gets the hint that I'm not going to respond. "All I meant was that you and Andrea aren't exactly married. If you don't love her, I just don't understand why you can't keep your mind open to someone you might. Because I know how you get. You get in these ruts because they're comfortable and you don't want to try for better. Because that'd take you out of your happy little Moira bubble."

When we reach the fairly steep hill that leads to Madeline's ancient stone-front house, I'm ready to scream at Bailey for being the worst friend of my life. My first relationship and she's trying to ruin it by supporting the feelings that I shouldn't be feeling.

Of course, I don't scream at her because I don't do conflict. Instead, I walk her right to the doorstep of her grandmother's house and say, "So, enjoy Madeline's cooking!"

She scoffs. "Ha, Grandma can't cook. Luna's making us this curry with homemade sauce and everything."

"Sounds good!" I sing, forcing a smile.

"Yeah, probably."

Then, out of nowhere, she hugs me. A real hug, not like her usual I-hate-this hugs. Warm and caring, like the kind normal best friends probably share. "I'm sorry, Moira."

"Huh?" is what comes out of my mouth. In my head, I'm gloating. *You should be sorry, you jerk.*

She just smiles. "This is the end of it, I swear. I am not my grandmother. I'll stop trying to run your life, okay?"

"Yes, please."

She rests a hand on my shoulder. "You have a good night, okay?"

"I will," I promise, my feet already shuffling in anticipation of rushing away from that house.

She gives me another real hug, and that's it. She goes inside and leaves me there in the dim blue twilight to argue with the echo of her words all the way home.

Chapter Nine

Bailey said that was the end of it, but it really wasn't.

Saturday morning, while Andrea is off doing lunch with her mother while also meeting her mother's new boyfriend— some high-profile environmental lawyer who also has a daughter—she has an idea. That dinner at Madeline's, or specifically the after-dinner tea her grandmother insisted on having, reminded her of the existence of Miho's, a little vegan teahouse down the road from my house. Now she wants us to go there, along with her Drama Camp coworkers.

I agree to her plan because I really like Miho's and, anyway, Layla will be there too. So the chances of Bailey pulling a sneaky hide-in-the-bathroom move to turn a meet-up into a real date are basically zero. Just a casual hangout with one of my best friends, a relative stranger, and a girl I find more interesting than I should, at a restaurant I'd visit more often if my dad wasn't a gourmet chef. Really, it sounds like the kind of thing normal people might do on a Saturday in July.

The teahouse is empty when we get there. Our server, a kind-looking Japanese guy who looks like he's probably in his midthirties, tells us we can sit wherever we want. Bailey expresses no preference. And Layla appears to be too wowed by the fact that the entire teahouse is built into a giant gazebo to answer. But I know where I want to go. Beyond the walls of the gazebo is a small patio that extends beyond the back of the structure. It's nothing fancy, but it does overlook a placid little marsh.

Millie, as it turns out, is staring in that direction too.

"They have tables out there," I explain, which settles it.

Things don't go exactly how I would like because Layla turns out to be some kind of teahouse guru, thus killing my delirious glee at the thought of recommending everyone the perfect tea to suit their preferences. Instead, our shaggy-headed, self-appointed teahouse ninja instructs everyone to get almond milk tea because it is literally impossible to mess up. Bailey and Millie go along with that like sheep with particularly bad taste, but I have my little pot of jasmine green anyway.

Everyone gets food too, but it has nothing to do with tea, so I barely notice what anyone is eating.

Not that I could comment on it if I did care. Turns out, Layla Foster is one of those girls who devour all of the words in a conversation. She's not boring—far from it, as she seems to have a little tidbit of knowledge for every topic ever—but it's not exactly the prime environment for getting to know Millie a little so that Bailey will leave me alone about that.

Layla chats on about comic books and silent films and French history and hats and whatever else comes into her head, until the wheel of random topics that is her finally lands on sexuality—specifically, hers. She describes lightly what being asexual is like, and how people always say she'll change her mind when she meets a nice guy or girl.

"But what they don't get is that I *want* to meet a nice guy or girl," she explains, her brown eyes animated. "One of my sisters says it's like being a kitten. Like, I just have no interest in sex, you know? But I still want to be held and cuddled and just, I don't know, loved."

"Honestly, that sounds pretty good," Bailey admits. "It'd put an end to all those agonizing 'Is it love? Is it lust?'

arguments that people have with themselves."

Layla shrugs. "Sometimes, yeah. But it's really hard to meet people who feel the same. And, since sex is kind of this undercurrent in daily life for everyone over sixteen, sometimes I feel left out. I just feel like such an outsider, you know?"

Millie slides her elbows forward on the table and takes a sip of her tea. "To be fair, Layla, you are kind of an outsider. I mean, even compared to us outsiders, you're pretty weird."

Everyone laughs at that.

That moment opens the floor to a bit less Layla-centric conversation where we all toss out our thoughts on what love even is.

Layla, who really does look like a bit out of place with her disheveled hair, wide eyes, and black t-shirt with a neon silhouette of a tap-dancing panda, offers up the cute idea that love is when you can be wrapped up in someone's arms and feel entirely at peace. She immediately follows that up by disclaiming she's never dated anyone but stands by it anyway.

Bailey, who in contrast has dated a lot, jokes that she believes that love exists, but that it probably isn't for her. She even confesses that she believes in the idea of each person being set to meet that one perfect match for them.

"Except people are too stupid and self-centered and cynical for it to work that often in real life," she clarifies.

Millie takes her time in coming up with her contribution. She stares at the table for a bit, looks at me, and then examines the tabletop again. Finally, she taps her straw—*What kind of self-respecting tea is served with a straw anyway?*—against her plastic cup and gives this little laugh that, when paired with her shy, teeth-baring grin, might be slightly charming.

Unlike the other two, Millie tells us a story. She admits she is a romantic, even though she really has no reason to be. Her parents are apparently the type of people who should have divorced years ago but never did because they didn't want people in the neighborhood talking about them. And her sister is basically an ice princess. She's never had a boyfriend but seems to get a thrill out of shutting boys down.

Then she half-smiles. "Heh, and my brother's been dumped so many times that it's strange that his country singing career hasn't taken off. So, yeah, not a lot of romantic examples coming from my real life."

She tells us the story of this girl she's been dreaming about since she was in first grade. "Never had a lot of friends growing up, and my family and I were never that close. But when I'd sleep, sometimes there'd be a girl who'd just take my hand and make me feel not lonely and, just, totally put together for once. I've been dreaming of her ever since, on and off—always that same girl. She's always my age, like she's growing with me. Like she's my shadow or something."

Bailey shoots me a quick glance that makes me want to dump almond milk tea on her head, then asks Millie, "What's this girl look like? Like, do you find her cute, or is she more like a big sister or something?"

"It's weird. I don't really know what she looks like. Maybe I forget or something, but I have no idea. I always know that it's the same girl because of the feeling I get when I see her. When she takes my hand, I don't feel so messed up. I feel like stuff will work out. To me, that's what love is. Stuff working out and just, I don't know, not feeling so messed up because someone's there for you."

She presses her hands into her forehead and lets out a long sigh. "Oh man, that sounded so much more profound in my head."

Layla rests a hand on Millie's wrist. "I think it's beautiful."

But Millie isn't having any of that. "Moira hasn't given

her take yet," she says, nodding like she's going to wait to be truly embarrassed until she's heard how weak my vision of love is.

It would be a good moment to unleash a cool, nonchalant, "I don't know," but the others are staring at me with wide, expectant eyes. Well, Millie is. Layla is staring at some far point behind my head, obviously a bit spaced out now that she's not speaking or being directly spoken to. And Bailey is just kind of half looking at me, as if she knows I'll give some evasive non-answer and is already disappointed in me for being such a wimp.

So I have to actually think about it, what love even is— even though I would prefer Layla to open her mouth and let loose another stream of words. No doubt what she knows about quantum physics is very interesting.

Seriously, this is harder than filming without a script. And way more pointless, because I am at least paid for my *Lunaside Girl* appearances. This is just blathering with friends. I want to pay the kindly Japanese guy and then get the heck out of here and go paint. Really, I want to see Andrea *and* paint, but she's still meeting her mom's mystery man. Are they talking about love over food too? Is Andrea getting all squirmy like I am? That thought comforts me, like we are somehow tethered.

I imagine my girlfriend, chatting with her fabulously un-middle-aged mother and "The Boyfriend," and suddenly I get caught up in that image, like I'm there with them, and I lose myself. Like being scenery drunk, without the scenery. Then words just tumble out of my mouth—thick, dribbling, accidental syllables.

"So, uh, I think love is when you realize you'll do anything for someone. Like, no matter what, no matter how impossible it is, you just love them and you deal with that as best as you can. You follow them around, make a fool out of yourself. Like you, I don't know, carry their books if you're fourteen, ride in their stupid tiny car with them even when you hate cars if you're older than that and, uh, I don't know."

I put my hands on my forehead, just like Millie did, and exhale. The difference between us is that I don't even think what I said sounded profound in my head. It just sounds stupid and like I just made it up and, worse, ripped it off entirely from Millie's recent book-nerding session.

"Heh, well said," mutters the ghost-eyed inspiration for that garbled excuse for a reply.

That's when Millie perks up and gets everyone chatting about their favorite books. It's a little less depressing than when she and Mom got going, but I still feel entirely outclassed. Now that I've heard her talk for more than five minutes, I'm not all that surprised that Layla has apparently read every book. What does shock me, however, is that Bailey knows about three-quarters of the books Millie rhymes off, and she's somehow heard of Sir Philip Sidney.

"Um, Bailey?" I ask, wanting to be part of a conversation I have no business being a part of. "You read things that aren't fashion magazines?"

She looks at me and shrugs. "Duh, I'm, like, in love with Renaissance fashions. Where else do you think I'd get proper descriptions of that stuff? *Modern* books? Movies?"

Another major surprise is how well Millie is handling being the center of this conversation. She's sitting up straight, with her hands held together on the table, her whitish eyes fixed thoughtfully on whoever is talking at any given time. She just looks confident. Well, she doesn't *just* look confident. Sitting there with that messy, starkly black hair that hasn't been combed since at least yesterday, and that summery white tank top that shows off her soft arms and that shapely chest, she looks, well, hot.

That is a problem. I want to ask her, "Hey, Millie, do you think maybe you could throw on a raincoat and maybe not be so interesting? I kinda need you to be a bit more resistible right now. Thanks for understanding."

But that doesn't happen. She keeps being her shyly vibrant self even after we pay and head back toward the camp, with Bailey and Layla walking ahead of us. For once, I'm not furious at my friend for blatantly setting me up to cheat on my girlfriend. She has a pretty decent excuse for ditching me. Layla had grabbed Bailey's arm and started telling her about the summer she spent in Milan with her parents and five sisters, which included a visit to some fashion show for up-and-coming designers.

Bailey's jaw dropped into the dirt, and questions flew out of it like tiny moths, all darting for the light that was Layla's DIY-maned, knowledge-filled head.

One of which was, understandably, "You, at a fashion show? Seriously?"

So I hang back with Millie and try to ignore her dusky voice as she goes on about books, before moving on to the Trundle Island scenery, describing scenery drunkenness in such perfect detail that all it lacks is Andrea's cutesy label. And listening to her voice is kind of like *being* scenery drunk, so I try to pretend it's Bailey talking. Or Jude.

I loved Judith deeply at one point, but I've never found her loud, sharp, achingly jockish voice attractive. It's like having a conversation with an anthropomorphic megaphone sometimes.

But even if I get over Millie's voice, let alone what she's saying, there's still the fact that she is walking very closely beside me. So closely that we are almost touching. We aren't, because we've both adopted the same I-want-to-touch-you-but-I-can't hand-on-elbow pose, so that our nervous knuckles are facing each other—mirror images

We are standing very, very close, and Millie is very, very attractive. Even her smell—grass, sand, and nondescript soap—gives me a tingle.

My mind becomes a white wash, nothing but foam. Like

a broken and finished wave, I am slipping out, going with the tide. Instinct guides me. Instinct, and the pull of this thoughtful girl, who likes nature and books and who has perfect, natural curves and who smells like a lawn that's next to a beach.

I reach out the hand that was just before trapped by my other hand and find her similarly trapped hand. I don't have the courage to look her in the eye as I do it, but I imagine I would see surprise registering in her ghost eyes. But she reciprocates. She lightly wraps her fingers in mine, and it feels like a shock.

We say nothing else for that entire walk. I have no idea what Millie is thinking now, but I spend the entire time trying to convince myself how normal this is.

Girls holding hands is a commonplace thing, I tell myself, invoking Mom's therapist voice as we meet some old couple who doesn't even blink as they pass us. *It is a perfectly acceptable symbol of friendship in our culture.*

Of course, I have to admit, in my own voice, *most girls don't get that much of a thrill out of it. And, if they did, they certainly wouldn't be feeling like this with someone who isn't their girlfriend while said girlfriend is off being a proper daughter at some family thing.*

But I don't let go until we make it back to Lunaside. Because: A) I don't want to make some big scene about it, and B) it feels so great that I physically can't break it off until the last possible second.

After I do, though, I hole up in my cabin, letting guilt wash over me like mud. How can I do this to Andrea? To Millie? Me, who still has trouble admitting I have a sexuality at all? How have I suddenly become this wild woman with no morals who just holds hands with whatever girl while my girlfriend is away?

I grab my phone out of my bag and type quickly.

Andrea, are you still meeting Mystery Boyfriend? I need a triple dose of you, and now.

Chapter Ten

Andrea replies sooner than I am expecting. In the back of my mind, I sort of hope that it's more to do with how badly she wants to see me than how terrible her mother's boyfriend is. Either way, though, as the sun is going down, I get a reply.

Would love to meet. Mom and Aidan are staying in. Can take car. Meet at your house?

Aidan, huh? Assuming there is only one Aidan on Trundle Island who practices law and has a daughter, *that's* interesting. I tell her yes.

Andrea replies like the scheduling maven she is.

What time?

With shaking fingers, I reply.

Now's good.

Realizing both how desperate that likely sounds and how impossible it is to take it back now that it has been sent, I throw my phone in my bag and head home.

When I get in the door and see Mom at the table, scribbling in a notebook, my heart sinks. Somehow, I know I can only have the moment I want with Andrea if the house is empty. I'm brave enough to hold hands with some girl who isn't my girlfriend, but I'm still not that brave.

"Hello, Moira," Mom says, continuing to scribble without looking at me.

It is then that I notice the dark, earthy aroma permeating

the air. In normal houses, the smell of brewing coffee is no doubt a comforting staple. Here in the Connell house, where the coffee is kept solely for guests and for when Dad can't wake up at four in the morning for work, it is the scent of an alien world.

I squint at the white cup beside Mom's notebook. "Mom, are you drinking... coffee?"

"Yes. I'm just compiling some notes, just thoughts and things. I thought it'd keep my mind focused."

"Those must be some notes," I comment.

She smiles and looks up at me. "You could say that, yes. But I suppose I could take a break. My eyes are beginning to lose focus, and frankly this coffee is atrocious."

"Ha, well, I could have told you that."

As if to prove the point even though I agree with it, Mom takes another sip of the coffee and sticks out her tongue. "Blegh, just awful. So then, would you like some tea?"

Even though Andrea is probably on her way, I am kind of thrilled that Mom has asked me to sit with her in a totally normal motherly way, the way she sometimes did before that first dinner with Andrea.

"Of course," I have to answer.

So we each get out our little ceramic pots that we only use for our all-time favorite teas—Mom's is a specific oolong blend that she orders online, and mine is my usual jasmine green—and have tea together for the first time in at least four months.

We don't talk much at first because living in the same house as someone and going as long as we have without talking one-on-one is the kind of thing that makes conversations hard.

Soon enough, though, Mom taps her notebook and says, "I've been thinking about scripts lately."

I raise an eyebrow. "Scripts? Like, uh, film scripts?" Neither of us have ever been much for movies.

She shakes her head. "No. More like behavioral scripts. Like the expectations we hold for how we think situations in our lives will go. Know what I mean?"

I reply that I only sort of do.

Taking a sip of her tea, Mom turns her brown eyes on me, some spark of an idea flashing across them as she speaks. "Yes, well, I've been thinking about how parents hold these life scripts for their children. We're all guilty of it, but we might not necessarily know that until those scripts are violated. For example, a child who becomes a playwright in a family of doctors, a son who grows up and becomes a priest when his parents wanted him to carry on the family name, or—"

"A daughter who doesn't have a five-year plan and also happens to like girls?" I reply, a little surprised that I caught Mom's line of reasoning so fast.

"In-indeed."

Simultaneously, we take a steadying gulp of tea.

Mom stares at her notebook and then continues. "Your decision not to go to university upset me much more deeply than your coming out did. I'd always envisioned both of my children graduating high school and then continuing on to university right away. And I suppose I'd also imagined that, yes, you'd meet a guy along the way. So when you introduced Andrea to me, it was like you destroyed the last vestige of my plans for you. However, I admit that meeting Millie made me ponder the issue a bit more deeply."

"Millie? Why?"

"I never knew what to say to Andrea. With Millie, the conversation flowed a bit more freely because she was more the type of, hmm, partner I'd envisioned for you, male or female. That was when I came upon that idea that, perhaps, it was my life scripting that was getting in the way."

"But Millie's not my anything, Mom. We're friends, but that's it. Andrea and I are still together," I explain, hating that the distance that has emerged between us means that I have to explain that at all.

She takes another long drink of her tea. "Nevertheless, my point about life scripting remains salient. I hope you understand that I am making the effort."

"I know," I sigh. Compared to Millie's "get out of my house" mother, Mom is practically a hero. It doesn't make her any less frustrating to deal with in reality, though.

My mother has no response but seemingly can't bring herself to get back to scrawling in that notebook of hers, so we just drink our tea in silence. After about five agonizing minutes of that, there is a single knock at the front door.

"Andrea!" I shout to no one.

Politely excusing myself from the table, I stride toward our front door. An involuntary "whoa" escapes my lips when I see Andrea standing there.

No doubt she jumped right in the car right after getting my text, without thinking to dress down from her dinner date, because this is not a side of her I've ever seen. For one thing, she isn't wearing a sweater vest. She's replaced it with a much more stylish combination of a deep purple button-down shirt with a black fitted sweater worn over it, so that only the collar and the cuffs are visible. Her hair is also masterfully gelled for once, as if she's found a stylist who can work with her cowlicks rather than try to hide them. This is all topped off by purple gem stud earrings, a subtle touch that radically alters her look.

It's as if the Andrea in front of me has no connection to that tiny little geek who tries to dress like an old man but winds up looking like a little boy. She stands up straighter and just generally exudes a more adult charm. Seeing her like this gives me a sudden welling up of a feeling that is warm and wavelike, a rising tide on a sunny day.

I grab her hand and pull her inside. "Hi."

"Hey," she breathes.

Of course, Mom is still there when we get back into the kitchen. She tells me to sit, then invites Andrea to do the same. Now that we've had our little tea moment, I could have just as easily told her that we were busy. At this point I don't think I even care about whether or not my girlfriend and I are alone in the house. Unfortunately, Andrea's chronic politeness decides that we'll be sitting with Mom.

To be fair, it starts well. Mom starts asking Andrea what it's like to be an only child. She politely answers that she has no point of comparison but doesn't feel lonely or anything. It's such a relaxed conversation that I'd normally be overjoyed to see it. As it is, I impatiently shift in my seat as I watch them—a silent, fidgety mass of I-want-Andrea-now-please.

Still, it's pretty great until Mom starts talking about her adventures studying birth order as a graduate student, pedantically admitting that, "Although we found no significant differences between the only children and those with siblings—and indeed between those born at different points in their family's birth order—in our research, I always felt that only children sought parental approval through organization and achievement, not unlike the oldest children in our study. I always felt that these, ahem, nerdish traits emerged from a closer relationship to the parents."

I press my palm into my eye. Did my mother just call my girlfriend a nerd? I mean, she is—no secret there—but, really?

"Oh, that's interesting!" Andrea comments, either too nice or too oblivious to realize what my mother has just said.

Mom nods quickly. "Mm-hmm, well, as I've said, we did not find significance. But I think if I was still in academia, I'd reattempt that study."

"Well, I'm sure you'll find something eventually," Andrea says, smiling with her eyes. She uses that trick on me sometimes when my artistic self-esteem crashes, and it totally works. A few seconds of that, and I feel like I'm the greatest artist who ever lived.

Mom seems to feel the same way. She smiles back at Andrea. A warm, eye-crinkling smile that, for a second, makes her looks entirely at ease with the fact that she is having a relatively normal conversation with my girlfriend. Well, normal for her anyway.

The moment doesn't last long. Eventually, she casts her eyes back down to the table and clutches her notebook. It seems like bashfulness from Andrea's attention, rather than her usual straight-up disapproval of her, but it still kills the conversation. It isn't long before she puts her teapot away and excuses herself to her bedroom to "jot a few notes, do a bit of bedtime reading and such."

But it feels sort of like progress, so I tell her good night with some satisfaction. Then, when she's closed the door to her room, I enclose Andrea's tiny, pale hand in my comparatively gigantic one and whisper, "Uh, sorry about that."

She smiles bashfully. "I was really surprised to get your text. It was so... forward."

"Yeah, well." I shrug, because there's no reasonable way of explaining what had inspired me to write it. "You look totally stunning, by the way. I'm glad you rushed here."

"Of course I did! Do you have any idea how long I've waited for you to text me late and tell me to come over so you could have me right now?" She giggles.

"Uh, about four months?"

Andrea's "Things I Hope to Do with My Girlfriend (Moira)" list definitely has a box that says "Get Asked to Come Over in the Evening." The thought makes me grin until my considerable overbite is no longer a topic for debate.

"Yeah, about that long," she whispers, squeezing my hand.

***

As we soon as we're in my room, Andrea shuts the door and turns off the standing lamp beside my bed. There is at least part of a moon tonight, and it gives the room a calm, warm ambience which makes me swoon.

Andrea quickly wraps her arms around me. I lean forward, hoping that an entire day's frustrations and complications can be obliterated by a kiss. They can't, but it still feels pretty liberating to be free of the usual fear that comes when we do stuff like this. Like maybe whatever I do here in my room with my girlfriend is safer than the alternative. It really makes me feel sort of bold, like I'm the kind of person who is capable of totally satisfying, not-at-all-messed-up intimacy.

Without thinking too much about it, I move my fingers to the bottom of Andrea's sweater. She looks up, seemingly surprised.

"Moira," she breathes. "What?"

"I'm deformalizing you," I blurt, with a stupid-sounding matter-of-factness that would have killed the mood for anyone who isn't us.

The look in her eyes could probably be described as shock. And rightly so. Since we've been together, I've never initiated anything this involved. It's possible I'm about to change that.

Possible, but unlikely. I get as far as removing her sweater, leaving her definitely silk shirt intact, before my mind starts wandering. What if Mom stops in to remind me that I've left my tea stuff on the table? What if things get a bit too good, and I accidentally confess what happened earlier?

Stupid thoughts, but no less halting for their stupidity.

Andrea seems to pick up on what's happening. She grabs

my wrists, smiles comfortingly, and whispers, "We don't have to. Besides," she adds, leading me toward the bed, "I'm still riding high on that text."

So we don't. Andrea scurries off to my closet and hands me a pair of my pajamas, while making sure to tease me about wearing pajamas in July. I put them on and bury myself in my bed's wine-colored comforter. Then she undresses and comes back in one of my t-shirts, which falls to about her knees, and hops into bed too.

Less than a second after, she presses herself into me and kisses me with an overpowering confidence that throws me out of reality. For the moment, she ceases to be the five-foot-nothing girl with the double-digit weight who's somehow gotten me to the point where I can enjoy a night in bed with her. As she gently does her thing, cautiously and carefully caressing my very-much-clothed self, I am the one who feels dwarfed.

Unrestrained by worries and anxieties and shyness as she is, there just seems to be a whole lot more of her in the room than me. Compared to this tiny little nerd whose only point of anxiety in life is that she wanted a girlfriend, I feel particularly messed up and very small. She is infinitely sweet for accommodating me, but likely I don't deserve her. Of course, I'll be selfishly keeping that fact to myself.

Because her intensity feels amazing. Under her quietly confident hand, all those complications and all my neuroses release themselves in breaths and sharp laughs and noises I'm not sure I make until suddenly there is just nothing. No anxiety, no me being a heartless jerk with no morals, no strained mother-daughter relationships, no stupid, stubborn best friend who can't leave me alone, no Millie. Just darkness, and the quiet hum of my everything.

Chapter Eleven

Since there were obviously other things on my mind the night I had Andrea over, I never did resolve whether or not Andrea's mother's Aidan was Aidan Hanley. It didn't occur to me to ask Andrea until she'd headed out the next morning, after getting a text from her mom to see if she'd like to have dinner at "Aidan's" and meet "The Daughter." Then I forgot about it again. I didn't really care, but part of me liked the idea of my girlfriend and me potentially having that odd little connection. Like now we could bond more deeply because we shared the same always-in-a-hurry, silk-shirted Zodiac sign.

So another week of camp started without me hearing from Andrea whether or not "Aidan and The Daughter" meant the Hanleys, but that was okay. Jeremy had informed me that I had more important Monday morning thoughts. Like how there is a country in Africa called Senegal. They mostly speak French, apparently.

Jeremy, no closet fan of food in general, had decided that *The Lunaside Girl* desperately needed a cafeteria episode. So he got Martin, the guy running the Lunaside cafeteria— who is originally from Senegal, which is why we got our geography lesson—to do it. Martin was one of Dad's favorite interns at the resort; he got him the Lunaside job as a chance to get him closer to realizing his dream of basically doing what Dad does. In a bold move, Martin called up my father, who originally started the cafeteria thanks to Madeline's insistence on having a "famous TV chef" involved with her camp, and asked if he'd appear on camera too.

In a bolder move, Dad told him he would.

So this morning we end up learning about Martin's home country and how he moved to Trundle Island because he wanted to study at our culinary school—which is apparently one of the best in the world—while we wait for Dad to show up. In the spirit of that, I'm putting my campers to work drawing maps or flags for countries either real or imagined. Shapiro opts out almost immediately, which is fine because that's basically the standard now. The only unsettling part is how happy she seems with refusing.

"Oh, I think your idea is brilliant!" she sings with eerie charm. "But I've got a better one, so I'd rather do that, if it's okay."

What unnerves me the most is that my approval suddenly matters to her, but I decide to shake it off and ask Martin about his knowledge of vegan cooking.

Dad thunders through the cafeteria double doors not long after we've started chatting, still wearing his chef's uniform. He nods familiarly at all of my campers as if they're his nieces and nephews, puts his arm around Jeremy like he's his son, and buries his actual daughter in a bear hug from behind.

Then he looks down at Andrea, who is holding a microphone, and smiles awkwardly. It isn't the same kind of awkwardness as Mom's; Dad's always been awkward and strange around girls who are not me. And also I think it's just logistics. Dad's a very large man, both horizontally and vertically. Likely, he still doesn't know how to interact with Andrea's tiny self. But eventually, he decides to ruffle her cowlicks, which makes me smile.

"Just tell me what to say, and I'll say it," Dad declares, giving Jeremy a solemn professional-to-professional nod.

Our director pulls out his ponytail, studies the floor, then reties his hair and looks at my father. "Well, uh, Mr. Connell, since you're an expert—"

Dad holds up his large, reddish hands. "Hold on now, you've got both my daughter and my future daughter-in-law working for you, so I'm—"

"Dad!" I shout, feeling my face turn as red as my hair.

He winks at me as he shakes Jeremy's hand. "So, yeah, call me Ewan."

"Will do," Jeremy replies. His face twists in what is no doubt an effort not to laugh at Dad's—admittedly successful—attempt to embarrass me.

Once everyone gets to work, everything goes pretty smoothly. Dad's TV experience clearly hasn't left him. He effortlessly answers my series of tedious, uninspired questions featuring such gems as "So, what made you want to be a chef?" before just throwing out random anecdotes, like why there's one dish on his menu for each member of our family.

"The original was the 'Pasta Moira,' because my darling daughter here quit meat one day when she was sixteen and wanted to go vegan. My wife didn't want her doing that, but she resorted to living off rice and raisins to show she meant business. I thought a bit about it, cooked up a batch of egg-free penne along with fresh vegetables in a creamy—turns out, tomato plus coconut milk equals cream—garlic sauce and some vegan parmesan substitute that I bought from a local health food store. My daughter said it was delicious, and I never looked back."

He explains that the "Rory Deluxe"—basically an open-faced chicken sandwich with a tomato cream sauce and grilled veggies—appeared on the menu soon after because my brother grew a bit jealous of all the attention I got and declared he was going to eat nothing but chicken. Dad told him, "Eat nothing but chicken all you want, but you still gotta eat your vegetables."

Then he scratches his ear and quietly admits that the less said about "Mousse Cake a la Philoméne," the better because he copied it wholesale from Mom's grandmother's recipe, then named it that to appease her when she found out.

"But my wife's no pastry chef. She wasn't using it," he tries to explain, before turning it over to Martin.

Martin, who smiles shyly when I ask him to introduce himself, admits that he is not that comfortable talking for the camera. He insists that he's much more comfortable *doing* something for the camera.

Since Jeremy seems to think that we need another "action" sequence, as if Jude's training regime hadn't been enough excitement for a million webisodes, we follow Lunaside's resident chef into the kitchen as my dad politely excuses himself.

"Would love to watch you folks work," he explains, mostly to Jeremy, "but there's never a time when I don't feel like my staff's going to burn my restaurant down if I'm not there babysitting them."

So we film Martin doing his thing while I try to ask him some basic questions. He tells us that his mom was the one who got him to go to culinary school.

"She said to me, 'Maybe if you go to school, then you will make the food sing, rather than just moping around the house dreaming about it.'"

After I chuckle at that, Martin, who apparently wasn't kidding when he said he didn't like talking on film, holds a frying pan toward me and says, "Maybe you could make one? For the camera."

"One what?" I look down. There is a bunch of light brown goop in the pan.

"It's a pancake. I know you're vegan, but are you against working with eggs?"

I want to say yes, but I'm not sure if that would be the

truth. I just don't want to do whatever it is he's talking about. But I still say, "Uh, no," because having both a camera and a frying pan simultaneously pointed in my direction apparently makes me frustratingly agreeable.

He wants me to flip the pancake, as it turns out. I question the logic of making pancakes after ten in the morning, regardless of how dramatic of an "action" scene it might be, but I attempt it anyway. He shows me how to do it—which I can't help thinking will make for great footage—then lets me try. It doesn't seem all that hard, and I'm pretty confident that I can at least make my pancake fly into the ceiling and stick there forever or, failing that, flop onto the floor.

Interestingly, when I follow through just like Martin told me, neither happens. In some tragic violation of gravity, the batter just sort of explodes and ends up on me, my sundress, Martin's bald head, Andrea's hair, and Jeremy's camera.

As politely as I can, I excuse myself to go get cleaned up.

***

Once I get myself looking presentable again, I lead my campers back to our spot on the grass. I don't officially let Film Camp know I'm leaving, but I know my directors will understand.

I smile at my group like the pancake fiasco had never happened. Or at least that it had happened to someone else. Then it'd probably have been funny. "So how is everyone getting along with their geography stuff?"

"Awesome, actually!" Emma exclaims, holding up this inspired, yet very unfinished, drawing of the world with various bugs drawn over certain countries. I can name barely any of them, but she seems happy enough to explain them all. Cockroaches get to be in South America because that's apparently where the domestic ones are thought to come from.

Neil doesn't answer but shyly holds up his page. At the
top of it is a Japanese flag, with a heavily shaded picture
of a wave occupying the rest of the paper. It looks familiar
enough that I ask, "Is that the Great Wave?"

He nods. "Yeah! My grandmother is from Japan, and her
Great Wave scroll is one of the only things she took with her
when she left the country. Since Mom's a marine biologist,
the picture has kind of been passed down, like a family
symbol or something. It's important to us."

I tell him it's wonderful, in an even-handed way that
hopefully doesn't make me sound like I'm playing favorites.

Next, I think Terrence is trying to show me the skull-
covered flag that is to be the homeland of some tyrant villain,
his yet-unnamed creation of the day, but he is quickly shut
down when Shapiro literally shoves her drawing book in my
face.

"What do you think?" she asks, even though the book
is close enough that the drawing is just a blur of black and
white.

When I hold it at a more manageable distance, I see
that Shapiro has drawn tiny hearts all around the page, an
excruciatingly detailed border that leaves almost no white
space at all. Inside this heart-square, she's drawn two people.
Presumably a couple, because they are holding hands and I
guess also the hearts. At first glance, I see a girl and a guy.

The guy is dressed in a nondescript shirt and pants and
has an absolutely awful asymmetrical haircut, depicted by
haphazard black lines streaking off the boy's head, down
and to the left. The girl has long, curly hair and is wearing a
sundress with some elaborate geometric pattern. She's about
twice the size of the boy, who I suddenly realize is absolutely
not a boy and—

Oh my god. Me and Andrea.

I flash back to my earlier wonderings about Aidan and the
Mystery Daughter.

Mystery solved, I guess.

Although my hands are suddenly shaking with anxiousness, I'm not necessarily upset with Shapiro. As insufferable as she can be, she's just a kid. A pretty observant kid, but it's not like she would've drawn something like this without someone putting the idea in her head. Besides, her proportions really are improving quite quickly; it would be hard to be mad at her when she's so obviously learning from me.

But then I notice that she's written "true love" in delicate cursive at the top of the page and freeze. "Petrified from embarrassment" would be an understatement.

"Shapiro." I cough, unable to finish that with either praise or reprimand or with any words period.

She leans toward me and smiles perkily. "Andrea told me all about you two! I met her this weekend! She's Dad's girlfriend's daughter! Isn't that interesting?"

"Hmm, yeah," I reply. "It's interesting."

I calmly hand Shapiro her drawing book and calmly take a calm, calming breath. Calmness, I am the definition of it. After all, Shapiro Hanley is the sort of kid who makes people do funny things. Maybe for Andrea that includes disclosing the details of her romantic life even though that'd make things difficult for a certain camp counselor.

It's not as though my girlfriend decided to have a sit-down with an eleven-year-old to teach her all about lesbian relationships, especially knowing how I feel about that sort of openness. No, she likely has an explanation. A good explanation that starts with "Sh," ends in "piro," and has an "a" in the middle. I'll simply have to ask her about what happened, hear her side, and then we can laugh about our shared difficulties with Shapiro Hanley.

So I'm calm. Very, very, very calm.

I remain so calm that when I finally meet up with Andrea in front of my cabin at the end of the day, I find myself shouting, "Andrea! You told her! Why?" and then calmly collapsing into a heap on the ground.

Okay, not that calmly. Okay, not calmly. *At all*.

She gingerly lowers herself to the grass beside me. As usual, she's wearing black pleated dress pants, which she probably doesn't like getting dirty. I appreciate that she'd do that for me. Not that it makes me forget what she's done.

"Shapiro didn't need to know about us," I snap, even as she's lightly resting her small, warm hand on my shoulder.

Her comforting little hand shoots to the ground and starts tearing up handfuls of grass. Not good.

"Mom and Aidan are getting really serious," she mumbles. "That's why she decided it was time for me to meet him. And they both thought it'd be great if Shapiro and I could get along, because she's the kind of kid who's too precocious to have many friends her own age. I really like them both, and they're a part of my life now, so I feel they should know things about me. And, uh, I know you like to pretend otherwise, but you're kind of a big part of that."

What she's saying makes sense. Unlike me, Andrea is out there, living in the real world where she's encountering new people and new experiences. I can't expect her to live some not-quite-life where she has to lock down the fact that she has a girlfriend when she doesn't want to do that.

But knowing that doesn't stop the words from being ripped out of my mouth, like so much grass. "Oh, please! I'm 'a big part of that'? What about your film stuff? You've got lots to say on that too. You just want people to know that you have a girlfriend so you can go for that big reaction with every single person you meet! In fact, if you weren't so loud-and-proud about being with me, maybe Mom would have accepted us right away!"

In my head I add, *The way she accepted Millie.*

Her grass-ripping hand goes limp, as she seemingly loses the will to do even that. "I-I—" Her head droops into her waiting hands. Uh-oh.

She attempts a deep breath. But broken up as it is by obvious sobs, I'm not sure it counts as one. "Okay, I get that you're upset," she says. "But I can't stop being who I am any more than you can. And don't get me wrong. I love the way you are! It's just that I'm not reserved like you. When people are important to me, I need them to feel included in my life. I don't keep secrets, and I-I really thought Shapiro would be a safe compromise. She's such a bright girl, and she thinks very highly of you."

"She drew a picture of us," I grumble. "In her drawing book. She drew a picture of you and me holding hands."

"Cute," Andrea chuckles.

"It said 'true love' at the top." I sigh.

She stares at me with those big, innocent blue eyes of hers, which definitely reflect the approaching sunset just a bit more than usual. "Moira, listen. I really like being with you! But, like, part of that for me is being able to squeal with glee at people I care about that I have the most awesome girlfriend in the world, just like I do with film stuff. I'm the kind of person who knows what I want, and when I get it I can't hide my excitement! But then I remember how that upsets you, and sometimes I wonder..."

"Wonder what?"

"I don't know. I just think about stuff, you know? Weird stuff, I guess."

"Huh?" I ask, genuinely not following.

She shrugs. "It's stupid probably."

"Well, what is it?"

"Sometimes I just worry if I'm, like, enough for you, you know?"

"*What?*" Now I'm the one eradicating Lunaside's grass population. "That's ridiculous!"

And really, it is. Andrea is more than enough for me. *I'm* the one who can't just be happy with my cute, totally loving girlfriend.

"Okay, fine, but it isn't just that," she admits, her voice sounding a little ragged. "It's, like, I asked you out. Since you're the first girl to ever agree to go on a date with me, I was just riding so high on that at first that I didn't really think about what could go wrong. Then, I don't know, I got to see how you act when I try to do couple stuff, and I started feeling like maybe you're closed off like this because, well, you just don't want to be with me. But you're also too nice to dump me?"

Seeing exactly where she's coming from as I do, while also knowing what she hopefully doesn't about how I feel about Millie, makes my throat almost close over with what is sure to be the hugest sob in history if I let it escape. "Andrea, you goof! I'm not *that* nice! Also? I'm with you because you're the cutest geek I've ever met, and you make me smile just by being nearby."

Andrea giggles, just like I'd hoped, but she bites her lip like she's trying to hold it in.

I rest my hands on her shoulders. "I'm with you because you're you. I can't make it any clearer than that."

She stands up suddenly, brushes the back of her pants, and then laughs. "This isn't how I imagined this evening going. Aidan asked me if I'd babysit Shapiro tonight, because she really needs a steady babysitter, and I said I would. I spent all day waiting for the chance to ask you to come with me, but—"

I picture Andrea's "Things I Hope to Do with My Girlfriend (Moira)" list again. Somewhere on there is probably "Babysit Some Kid as a Couple." The box beside it is unchecked, forlorn.

That trapped sob grows heavy, suffocating. There's no question now; it's coming out. I am going to cry.

"'Bye Moira, I'll text you to say good night," she assures me, in a sunny-yet-grudging tone, before walking back to her cabin, leaving me to drown in my awfulness.

But drowning, as it turns out, is a lot harder than it seems. After only a few minutes of crying, all the awful fades, replacing itself in my head with my usual easy-mix blocks of guilt cement. Not pleasant, but familiar at least. I still want to cry bathtubs at how terrible I am at being a girlfriend, but I at least feel like maybe I'll get over it at some point.

Wanting to speed that process up, I go to the dune. I've never had to test its healing properties against such heady matters before. The only other time I faced this much sadness was after Jude rejected me, and I spent almost all of that week locked in my room, so the dune couldn't have saved me. I grab my drawing book, stuff it in my bag, and head down there, ready to lose myself in the impossibility of sketching waves in motion.

Except when I get there, I realize that probably isn't going to happen. My dune, for the first time in almost two decades, is occupied by someone who is neither me nor accompanied by me. I feel a warm surge of what I guess is territorial possessiveness, like maybe how one of Emma's beloved cockroaches feels when its dark, damp home is threatened. Reminding myself to ask my camper if cockroaches even have homes at all, I clench my fists and walk up to Millie, fully intending to tell her that she is sitting on my dune and that I have never needed it more than I do now, so she'll have to leave.

Unfortunately she turns around before I can do that, her face twisted in what looks like concern. "You okay?"

My fists unclench, and I drop uselessly into the sand beside her. "Uh, maybe?" After a pause, I admit, "Uh, actually? Not really, I think."

"Well, if you wanna talk, I'm here to listen," she says, with an encouraging smile that shows off dimples I didn't know she had. "I'm a pretty good listener. Probably fair trade for being such a crappy talker," she jokes.

Not wanting to reject her outright, I make up some story about how filming is getting to me and how I'm embarrassed about exploding a pancake in front of a camera. She offers a very hollow, "Cheer up, Lunaside Girl," because probably she doesn't believe that this is my problem anymore than I do.

But she stops trying after that. As a quiet person herself, she likely understands that some problems just can't be talked away. And I'm still crying a little, so maybe that scares her.

She doesn't lose the look of wanting to help, though. She just keeps gazing at me with that same sleepy-eyed smile that suggests she'll do whatever I ask. It makes me nervous, mostly because what I'd ask of her isn't something I want her to actually give. I want her close; I want her to cuddle into me, right here on my dune, regardless of who might see us.

She stares at me, and I meet her eyes. We don't say anything, but there seems to be something buried in that silence—a message. For a moment, I feel like leaning forward and kissing her would be the easiest, most natural thing in the world.

That moment quickly passes, and I wake up to the real world again. The real world where I have a girlfriend who cares about me, even though I'm making every effort to mess that up.

Millie laughs to herself. "You're so beautiful, Moira. I don't say that word a lot because it's cliché, but seriously. Inside and out, you've just got no idea. It almost makes me wish that you were—" She ends that deadly sentence with a sigh. A sigh, and a slow, noncommittal reaching out of her hand.

I quietly wrap my fingers around it, doing my best to ignore the tiny thunderstorms that have suddenly broken inside of me.

Chapter Twelve

The next morning, I wake up a half hour earlier than usual. My cement block of guilt has become a screaming, hissing, flaming-hot ball of self-disgust. Terrible, but it makes for a pretty effective alarm clock.

As soon as I open my eyes, I shoot out of bed. Nothing all that dangerous happened between Millie and me, other than the holding-hands thing. But I still can't forgive myself for the fact that I did that just after making Andrea cry, leaving her to deal with her issues alone. What kind of girlfriend am I?

I hurriedly throw on the forest-green version of the official camp t-shirt and a pair of emerald-green shorts that sort of match, just because I know it'll amuse Andrea. I then practically leap out of my cabin's front door, frantic to expend some of this nervous energy. That amounts to doing about eighty million laps around the Lunaside field, while wishing that Judith had never discovered the wonders of sand running just so I'll have company, until I see Martin unlock the cafeteria's front doors.

I sprint into the large building and keep running until I reach the lunch counter. "Hey! I know you're still setting up, but, uh, do you think I could get a large, black coffee?"

Martin shoots me a raised eyebrow and teases, "Never known you to like the stuff before. Does your father know about this?"

"It isn't for me," I scoff. "It's an emergency! Also, maybe do you have some kind of, I don't know, pastry-like breakfast thing?"

He gestures toward a tray beside the cash register, which holds various individually wrapped muffins, Danishes, and other things Dad donated from the resort that I wouldn't eat in a million years. "Sure, yeah, which would you like?"

"I don't know! I don't eat this stuff. What about that, uh, triangle thing? The one with the chunks of sugar on it?"

"The cherry turnover? You got it!" he replies, handing me the coffee and the pastry with a big, friendly smile. No doubt he's just excited not to be the only Lunasider in the cafeteria this early.

"Okay, thanks," I reply as I run out of the cafeteria and toward Andrea's cabin.

When I get there, I clear three of its four steps at once and throw open the door. Andrea appears to be deeply asleep, her face half-buried in her pillow. She looks kind of adorable like that, but now is the time for ruthlessness. I pull off her covers and roll her back and forth until she starts to make noises.

"I brought coffee!" I chirp, pressing the paper cup annoyingly into her cheek, "and some sweet thing. I'm sure it's probably wonderful and delicious and disgustingly nonvegan."

"Uh, you're sweet," she mumbles, her voice a little muffled by the pillow.

"No, this turnover is sweet. I'm just, uh, apologetic and also optimistic?"

"Moira, what—?"

"I'm really sorry about last night. I made you cry, and then I just let you go," I say, resolving to tell her about the stuff with Millie at some future point when things are absolutely smooth between us. Like maybe our twentieth wedding anniversary. "I am the worst girlfriend of all time, but I still felt that you deserved an apology. Plus," I add with a smile, "I thought if I plied you with pastries, you'd forgive me."

She immediately grabs the coffee and turnover and then laughs, "You goof, check your phone."

"My phone?"

I quickly pull the phone out of my bag. It tells me I have a new text message, which surely is how Andrea has decided to dump me. Swift and efficient—a dream breakup for her.

I close my eyes as I click it, and then open them.

Sorry about this evening. I overreacted. Gotta remind myself that you're just being you—never a bad thing. Forgive me?

I stare at the message. "Why are you apologizing? Were you having the same conversation I was?"

"I was," she replies as she rests the turnover on her stomach and starts sleepily picking at it. "I need to remember that you're just really shy. But it's hard because you're so comfortable in front of the camera."

"That's stupid. I'm comfortable in front of a camera because it's not really me. I just have to stand there and be the Lunaside Girl or Chef Ewan Connell's Assistant, and then I'm either told what to say or I don't say anything. It's not really about being outgoing like some people think it is."

"You're the perfect actor." She sighs. "You have no idea how many acting students would drop out of school right now if they could somehow harness the Moira Method."

I smile. "I'm glad to hear it, but I'd be happier if you could just realize that I like being with you, even though I won't yell it from a mountain or make out with you in public. I just like that side of myself to be something I save for someone really special."

Andrea slurps her coffee and then laughs. "Aw, what can I say to that?"

"Say that I can make it up to you somehow? Because I

still feel like throwing up from anxiety that you're going to dump me for being horrible."

"I don't know. You already brought me coffee and dessert for breakfast, even though you hate both."

"I just got those to wake you up. I'd at least like to give you a chance to show you that you can trust me when I say I care about you," I insist. "I-I really don't want to make you cry again, okay?"

"Technically, I made me cry with my bad thoughts, but there's still a way you could make it up to me, since you asked." She smiles mischievously from behind her coffee.

"Okay, I'll do it!" I say, feeling less like anxiety-vomiting already.

She confidently pops a piece of that awful pastry into her mouth and says, "I'm happy that you want to make it up to me so badly, but are you sure you want to agree to something without knowing what it is? I'll be sad if you back out now."

"As long as you aren't going to drive us to the nearest city and force me to kiss you on a busy street, I think I can handle it!"

"Oh, okay." She shrugs. "That's good."

"Wait. What was it you wanted me to do?"

"What's important is that you agreed," she says in an ominous voice that makes me feel as though I've signed away my soul. "I'll tell you later, but for now consider last night entirely forgotten."

"Wait, later? How much later? What did I just agree to?"

"You'll see," she sings, sounding more awake than I've ever seen her this early in the morning.

***

Because she's secretly a sadist, Andrea waits until Shapiro leaves on Friday evening to finally put me out of my misery. She comes up behind me, links her arm in mine, and says, "You'd better hurry and get out of those camp clothes! Aidan's a stickler for time, you know."

"What?"

She gives me an approving glance. "Just grab another t-shirt to go with those shorts. I don't get to say this very often, because of your love affair with sundresses, but you look very sexy as a proper camp counselor."

Undeterred by her idle flattery, I stomp up the steps of my cabin, yelling, "You knew I wouldn't have agreed to this if you'd told me beforehand!"

"It'll be fun," she calls.

"Oh yeah. *Fun*," I reply, when I step back outside.

"Nice." She smiles, seemingly pleased with my boring t-shirt. I've exchanged my forest-green Lunaside t-shirt for an emerald-green one that I mostly wear to bed because, although it fits well, t-shirts just aren't fun to wear. "But let's go! Mom left the car at the resort because Aidan will be picking her up there after we arrive."

I sigh in exasperation as Andrea starts on ahead, quickly passing her and arriving at the resort about a minute before she does. That gives me time to lean against her surprisingly tiny car and say, when she finally meets me in the parking lot, "Okay, so there's absolutely no way I am fitting into your short-people car."

She just laughs and pulls her keys out of her pocket. "Get in."

"Are you kidding? One of my legs would take up the whole backseat!"

"Well, tie yourself to the roof; you are not backing out now."

The car's ceiling ends up being higher than it looks from the outside, and the front seat moves all the way back. I don't have room to stretch or anything, but I'm okay. Still, that doesn't stop me from saying, "Hurry! I'll probably get arthritis or something because your car is discriminating against me."

"My car's pretty tolerant of people of most sizes; it couldn't have known that it'd have to hold a freakishly tall outlier like you."

"Shush," I say, folding my arms and legs in as I pretend to be more cramped than I am.

***

Aidan's cottage is at the end of a long dirt road with a thick wall of dark spruce trees on either side; their wide branches scrape Andrea's car as we pull into his yard. The moderately sized, perfectly square cottage is apparently built entirely out of logs and overlooks a wide, calm river, with a stand of silver birches growing out of the slope that leads from the cottage to the water. When we step onto the wooden deck that seems to go all the way around the house, I grab the rail to keep myself from swooning off of it.

Andrea knocks on the antique-looking wooden front door while I gape at the trees and the water. As impatient as Aidan Hanley seems to be, the kind of guy who'd choose to spend his summers here, let alone in a cottage that is basically a log cabin, is probably okay.

I start to fantasize about sitting on the deck near twilight, sketching the view of the water, but am quickly interrupted. Aidan answers the door just as he finishes buttoning his shiny, wine-colored paisley shirt and exclaims, "Andrea! Moira! Come in!" in a friendlier voice than I'm used to.

We follow him through the wooden-floored hallway, passing five mostly closed doors along the way, and head toward the large, open room at the end of it. He then turns toward me and says, "Shapiro's really excited that you agreed to come tonight, Moira. She adores you and your camp. And I personally think it's great for her to have you girls watch her. She's grown up around older adults like my parents and our neighbors down the road here, so she doesn't always get along with kids her own age, but she seems to like socializing with teenagers. I imagine that's healthier than only ever spending time with old ladies and me."

"Aw, well, she's a smart kid," I reply, deciding that it isn't a lie. "She's a very special person."

Aidan laughs and rests a hand on my shoulder. "You're probably a special person yourself for saying so."

He then confesses that he's sort of sneaking out on his daughter, because he and Andrea's mom are heading out to see a community production of Shakespeare's *Twelfth Night*, which is one of Shapiro's favorite plays.

That stuns me. Both of my parents dislike plays; Dad has trouble sitting still for long periods of time, and Mom's too afraid of crowds to enjoy something like that. And I didn't even know who Shakespeare was when I was eleven. I still don't know what *Twelfth Night* is.

Aidan tells us that, although we can reach him for emergencies, Shapiro isn't to know his whereabouts this evening. She apparently always gets upset when reminded of the fact that she happens to be eleven and not eighteen and thus has to go to bed at ten o'clock sharp, rather than whenever some evening outing ends.

"I go to bed at ten o'clock sharp," I point out.

"That is because you are strange," Andrea says, putting her arm around me.

Aidan laughs and then nods to us both. "So anyway, I've gotta finish getting ready. Shapiro's just reading in her room right now. She'll be fine in there. Just drop in and say hi every so often. Once she's finished with her book, she'll probably want to talk. You've both no doubt realized by now that she's quite the little chatterbox. Feel free to let her down lightly by putting on a movie; she knows not to talk during those."

He starts heading down the hallway but then turns on

his heels. "Oh, and Andrea? You've got my permission to dip into my secret stash," he adds with a wink, before disappearing into his bedroom.

"'Secret stash?'" I ask, squinting at Andrea suspiciously.

"Ice cream," she sings. "Aidan buys his at this local creamery that makes its own ice cream on-site. And they even use local, organic ingredients and—"

"I know about Crawford's Creamery," I remind her. "Dad and I did an episode about them? You'd think as our biggest fan you'd know that! But now, if you'll excuse me, I am going to sit by myself in the living room and try to forget that I am dating a girl with such a disgusting habit."

"Right. Well, suit yourself," she breathes, giving me a weirdly expectant smile as she drifts toward the kitchen.

When I get a good look at the heavenly paradise that Aidan calls a living room, I understand why she made that face. The entire back wall of the room is a series of patio windows, which lead onto the wooden deck and overlook a dark stand of spruce or something, and, of course, to the left is that river. With a sigh, I melt into the yielding black cushions of the Hanleys' couch.

By the time Andrea reappears, cheerfully toting a bowl that appears to contain, like, ten full scoops of some slimy-looking pink substance, I am too blissful to insult her wretched choice of dessert.

It is only when she shoves a spoonful of the stuff in my face and comments teasingly, "It's all organic too," that I snap out of my reverie.

"Um, I'm vegan? And even if I was thinking of giving that up, it wouldn't be for a pile of heavily salted and sugared frozen cream." I wrinkle my nose at the bowl and try to look revolted, but I keep almost laughing. That expressing our differing opinions on ice cream somehow counts as flirting to us is the kind of thing that makes me sort of smile on the inside.

Not on the outside, though. Because I really do find ice cream disgusting.

She frowns at her bowl but then shrugs and starts eating again. "Fine with me."

In other circumstances, I might find the idea of kissing, or at least cuddling, with my girlfriend next to such a stunning view to be almost tempting enough to risk being seen by the kid we are supposed to be babysitting. As it is, she's downing that ice cream so heartily that she is literally the least attractive person on the planet at this second. Plus, I'm not sure her kisses would be vegan anyway.

When Shapiro steps out of her room, in paisley pajamas that kind of resemble Aidan's shirt, I smile at her. At the moment, her presence is almost welcome. She serves as a convenient distraction from having to deal with seeing Andrea's grossest vice in action.

"Moira!" she yells, running over and sitting beside me on the couch.

I reach out and hesitantly hug her shoulders. "Hey, Shapiro, how are you?"

"Oh, I'm great. Reading got boring after I heard you guys come in, but, like, I didn't want to interrupt anything, so I didn't come into the living room right away."

"You weren't interrupting anything," I assure her.

She protests that she knows what teenagers are like, and that we don't have to hide it from her. Then she runs off to her bedroom, returning with an olive-green yoga mat, a couple of dolls, and a book, which she hands to me as she unrolls her mat and places the dolls on it.

"*Anne of Green Gables*. That's what I'm reading right now," she explains. "It reminds me of you guys and, since Andrea and I already have a game going that we started last time she was here, I didn't want you to get bored."

I look at the red-haired heroine on the cover and raise an eyebrow at Shapiro. I have read this book at least five times and, even if that hadn't been like ten years ago, I'd still have no idea what she's talking about. "What do you mean?"

She shrugs as she picks up one of the dolls—an olive-skinned one in a business suit, with short, dark hair that has been amateurishly cut. "It's not *exactly* you guys, I guess. I mean, you're really, really shy and Anne is not. But you're tall, not pretty, and you do have red hair. Plus, Andrea has dark hair and she eats a lot, so she's like Diana."

"Hey!" Andrea and I both shout.

She half-smiles as she hands the other doll to Andrea. It has long, red hair and is wearing a white dress that looks like it's been knitted by hand. "I just meant the love part. Obviously it was written, like, a million years ago, so they couldn't be *in* love, but they kind of love each other like you guys. That's why."

Having absolutely no response to that, I lean into the couch and flip through *Anne of Green Gables* while she and Andrea play with their dolls. Even as a kid, I'd never had much interest in dolls that I didn't cut out of paper, and only ever having Jude as a friend didn't exactly broaden my horizons in that way. It seems a little surprising that Andrea is playing along, as I'd have imagined that of the two of us I'd be more likely to play with dolls, but I'm not all that interested in the made-up lives of their made-up people.

That is until I catch a bit of what they are saying.

The red-haired doll's name is Maria. Evidently, she's a painter who spends a lot of time at the beach. The doll with the bad haircut is named Annie; she works on the set of some TV show. They live together on the olive-green yoga mat.

And, as it seems, maybe more than that.

When I start paying attention, Shapiro is in the process of leading the Annie doll back onto the yoga mat. "Hey, honey, I'm home."

Andrea gives me a look I can't define, then says, through Maria, "Oh, hey, I was just cooking dinner. It's all vegan and organic. Very healthy."

Was this how Andrea had told Shapiro about us? That seems a little less obnoxious than how I imagined it. In my head, she'd just walked up to Shapiro, shook her hand, and said, "Hey, you know your Art Camp counselor? That's my girlfriend."

This is different somehow; like it's easier to accept that she'd said it through Maria and Annie, rather than just blurting it out. But that could've been just my increasing fascination with this weird little doll game, and Andrea's part in it.

Here she is, sitting on the floor with an eleven-year-old, sipping cups of imaginary tea and eating imaginary vegan, organic food made by her doll's imaginary doll wife like it's the most natural thing in the world. She smiles kindly at all of Shapiro's suggestions for their game and speaks in a warm, big-sisterly tone that gives me this sudden, sort of heavy feeling in my chest. Like being punched in the heart, except great and not painful and terrible and however that would actually feel.

***

After Shapiro has packed up her dolls, and we've seen her off to sleep just after ten o'clock sharp, Andrea and I reconvene on the couch. She hasn't gone for more ice cream, so I put my arm around her and pull her close. She responds by nestling into my side adorably.

"This wasn't so bad, you have to admit," she says, sounding just a little cuter because her voice is half muffled by me.

"Yeah, it was okay," I reply, kissing her hair. "I enjoyed watching you play with the dolls."

"Oh yeah?" She yawns, moving out of her position in favor of putting her head in my lap.

"Yeah, it was like seeing another side of you. I've never imagined you as the type to play with dolls so, uh, naturally?"

She nods like she knows what I mean. "Well, it's not a side I got to let out that often when I was a kid. You know Mom; she's all business. And I guess I've just always wanted a little sister to play with, so there's that too."

I look down at my girlfriend and smile. None of what she said has ever occurred to me before. Up until now I've just assumed that her achingly professional ways are just a natural extension of her personality, like me and my artistic side. I haven't considered that there might be some small part of her that, like me, just really wants to relax and be allowed to do what she wants.

Maybe that explains her ice cream addiction.

That heart-punched feeling returns at the thought. To distract myself from it, I tap her on the forehead. "So hey, when you did get a chance to play with dolls as a kid, were they gay and married too?"

She laughs and sits up quickly. "Yours weren't?"

"Never played with that kind. I was too busy making them out of construction paper."

"Aw, and I bet they all had very pretty sundresses," Andrea lisps as she hops to her feet and holds out her hand.

"Huh?" I ask, taking her hand and letting her pull me to my feet. "You're not going for more ice cream, are you? And also, why would you need me for that? I am never going to support you—"

But she just stands on her tiptoes and puts a single finger over my lips. Then she quietly slides open the patio door at the end of the line of windows and leads me outside.

"Oh," I choke.

The view was nice enough when we'd gotten here earlier in the evening, and I'd seen it behind glass, but being here in it, on this mostly moonlit night, is almost too much. There's a light, warm wind coming off the river, hissing through the stand of birches that are themselves nothing but tall pillars of moonlight now. The dark spruce trees I saw earlier seem to blend with the ground so that everything past the house is a mass of black. Like nothing exists beyond this point.

I sigh and plop down on the edge of the deck, inhaling the heavy, nectar-like musk of the spruce trees.

Andrea quickly sits beside me. She puts her arm around me and chuckles. "Why'd you think I wanted you to come babysitting with me?"

A sudden wave of euphoria has stupefied my brain a little too much for a coherent reply. The best I can manage is a half-drunk sounding, "This?"

She moves in close, wrapping her arms around my waist. "Basically," she whispers, before kissing me deeply.

Normally, I would have been paranoid at a time like this. We aren't exactly safe and secure here. Maybe even less than at Lunaside. There are lots of ways this could end embarrassingly. Shapiro could wake up; Aidan could come home; some random neighbor could drop in to see if they could borrow a cup of olive oil or a slice of bread or something.

Except I'm not paranoid. All I can think of is the sight of Andrea playing with Shapiro in her caring, big-sisterly way and how she'd brought me here so I could get more scenery drunk than I've ever been in my life. That feeling in my chest strengthens, spreading throughout my body. Less like a punch now, more like a warm, slightly crushing, full-body hug on the inside that squeezes out all my thoughts, save for one.

Like an echo, Shapiro's voice reverberates in my head. *"They kind of love each other like you guys. That's why."*

For the first time ever, I put my hand behind Andrea's head and kiss her in the way she's no doubt been waiting for since we started dating. She lets out a breathless squeal of surprise, and then I pull her as close as I can and kiss her again, while quietly admitting to Shapiro's echo-voice that maybe she's right.

I can't speak for how Andrea feels about me, but maybe I've just realized that I kind of love her.

Chapter Thirteen

If I was a normal person, realizing I love my girlfriend is the kind of thing that would make a happy ending. Like putting the finishing touch on a really stubborn painting or something, it should make me feel gloriously, triumphantly complete. Of course, it doesn't. Because I am not a normal person. I'm a messy mass of guilt, anxiety, and self-disgust who passes decently as a normal person sometimes.

The way I see it, there are two major problems with my newly admitted love for Andrea. And I can't help but see them as a point-by-point list that'd make my girlfriend proud. It looks something like:

"Problems I Have with Loving My Girlfriend (Andrea)"

A) Andrea's shown no sign that she feels the same. Telling her could lead to Jude-class heartbreak.

B) Millie.

Because as convinced as I am that I love Andrea, my feelings for Millie haven't just magically disappeared. Seeing her still makes me tingle; being close to her still makes me want to be closer. And knowing that this makes me a terrible person who doesn't deserve to love anybody does not dampen the feeling all that much. Or at all, really.

Which is why I want to throttle Jeremy when he and Andrea show up on Wednesday to ask me if they can film the Drama episode. Surely he's gotten enough footage for at least ten webisodes now. Can't we just pretend Drama Camp doesn't exist?

The kind-yet-expectant look on his baby face tells me that no, we cannot do that. I'll just have to face the prospect of being codirected by the girl I love but can't tell. And obviously being on camera with the girl I really, really like but shouldn't. Stupid Jeremy and his stupid supernatural persuasion skills.

So we head to the cafeteria and get set up for the Drama webisode. I arrange my campers at the table in front of the stage. I tell them that they can watch Drama Camp's activities if they want but give them a lesson on figure drawing anyway.

"If you choose to do the activity, I'd like you to keep in mind what you know about basic model drawing. You already know that we always start with our basic skeleton—now I want you to think of that skeleton as an actual skeleton, with interconnected moving parts. Don't worry about giving your drawings too much detail for now; it's fine if you only get as far as drawing a figure in motion. All I ask is that, if you need a reference model, to focus on the counselors or me, only because if you were going to draw a particular camper, you'd need their permission."

Everyone but Shapiro seems satisfied with that and immediately fixes their eyes on Layla, who is at that moment hopping around the stage. Shapiro instead turns toward Andrea and smiles. "Hey, Moira, I can draw Andrea, right?"

Figuring that her "True Love" drawing is probably a one-time thing, I tell her she can. She immediately opens her drawing book and starts staring at my girlfriend. Kind of weird, but at least it means she won't be getting in the way of the filming.

With that settled, filming begins. Jeremy doesn't turn his camera on right away; he gives everyone a breakdown of what he wants to see beforehand. Expectedly, he wants another action scene, with the Lunaside Girl up on stage, getting involved in some Drama activity. He tells Layla and Millie to choose something fun looking and dynamic, but not that difficult. Presumably so that I can't have it explode in my face like so many hard-failing pancake flips.

Layla taps her chin dramatically and then scurries backstage with Millie and her entire camp trailing behind.

They reemerge in black outfits that look to mostly be the result of some thrift store searching. The kids are all barefoot and dressed in black sweaters, tights, jeans, and even sweat pants in some cases. Layla, for some reason, has on a two-sizes-too-large black hoodie and makes sure that everyone knows it with her ridiculous wannabe rap-star strut. Millie's wearing plain black pants—not unlike the ones Andrea wears on a daily basis—and a turtleneck.

I literally feel my breath stop in my throat.

She might as well be the first person to ever wear a turtleneck. Almost like anyone else who's ever worn one was just some wannabe beat-poet poser. It's fitted—was that Bailey's choice?—and shows off all of Millie's gentle curves. And its color matches the light-sucking blackness of her hair, which she seems to keep perpetually dyed as I've never seen her roots, in a way that accentuates her paleness and the ghostlike quality of her eyes.

Deep down I realize that this will be the only time in my life that I'll find a girl in a turtleneck unearthly beautiful. And I struggle with that, even as we begin our activity. I wrestle with it, try to focus on Layla as she leads everyone in a bunch of warmups that are much less intense than those torture methods that Judith calls "warmups." Wonderfully asexual Layla, who right now looks like a small child being eaten by a giant black kangaroo torso, and who guides us through stretches and breathing exercises like a professional.

Unfortunately, a whole ensemble cast worth of Layla could not make me forget that Millie is here too, stretching and breathing with the rest of us. And in that stupid turtleneck.

It's too much; I need escape.

I turn toward Andrea but immediately regret it. She smiles obliviously and gives me a thumbs-up, looking unquestionably adorable herself in a black-and-green argyle sweater vest, along with a white button-down shirt and her signature black pants. Recalling point A from my list, my stomach immediately floods with an army of angry, probably poisonous, butterflies.

Desperately needing some reprieve from my new job title of "hormonally charged teenager with no morals," I fix my gaze firmly on Jeremy. Sweet, gigantic Jeremy with his inoffensive light blue eyes, gorgeously perfect shoulder-length hair, and teddy-bear-like body. He is soothingly, comfortingly, calmingly unattractive. Possibly like a real teddy bear.

All that staring makes him order another take, but that's fine by me. By the time we get going again, I'm not so jolted by Millie's outfit or Andrea's general just-being-there-ness. I'm ready to do this.

"So, Layla, what activity did you have in mind? I'm up for anything," I declare with newfound determination.

She grins widely and claps her hands together. "Gosh, there are so many choices! I hate to pick just one but, hmm, if I had to I'd say, Famous First Words!"

"Famous First Words?" I ask, with a genuine ignorance that will probably make good webisode material.

Layla winks. "Yep! It's pretty simple, and it can get incredibly crazy!"

Then she runs to the back of the stage, raises her hands into the air, and yells, "Everyone, circle!"

The Drama campers and Millie dutifully arrange themselves into a giant circle that sort of automatically comes to include me.

Layla's eyes widen with excitement. "Now, Famous First

Words is one of my favorite games. You can use it as an icebreaker or during a play to learn lines or really anything. It's a simple game where one actor steps forward in some dramatic way," she explains, stepping forward and spreading her arms, "and then speaks a line. It can be a line from a play or just made up. The point is for the rest of the actors to continue it, either with the real next line or something else, until it gets to the original actor, who finishes the sequence with their original line. Make sense?"

Everyone, including me, nods.

I soon regret that confidence when a beaming Layla spreads her arms wide and says, "Why don't you start, Lunaside Girl?"

"Uh, I really don't think—"

"Come on, it's easy," Layla insists. "Let's hear your famous first words!"

I groan but can see no means of escaping. Still, I don't exactly feel up to playing along. In what I guess is a compromise, because it's just the straight truth delivered in a way that hopefully sounds harmlessly melodramatic, I step forward, put my hand on my heart, and say, "I am conflicted."

But Millie catches my eye for a second, and I know she's seen through that.

When it gets to be her turn, she mimics my tone, throwing her fists into the air and saying, "I want what I cannot have."

Since it's in the spirit of my overdramatic delivery, I'm sure no one else catches on to her meaning. But when it comes time to deliver my line a second time, it is a much more deflated, and dangerously real, "I am conflicted."

We go around like that, with Layla calling on some of her better actors to be filmed starting the circle. Then she calls on Millie, who fixes her eyes on me and says, "My love lives in shadows and dreams. When I wake, my love leaves."

Layla points out that this is two sentences, but the circle picks it up anyway.

The kids between Millie and me go with the dream idea and start adding lines about a love that is literally dreamlike, with ice-cream hair, a dress made out of pizza, and things like that. It's the kind of spontaneous, imaginative nonsense that my cautious mind is not made for.

When the kid next to me finishes telling the circle about how the dream love even likes video games and lets him win, I follow that up with a defeated shrug, saying, "I'm conflicted?"

That gets a few laughs.

The campers after me continue adding increasingly ridiculous qualities to the dream love until it is Millie's turn again. She winks at me, takes a dramatically deep breath, then turns toward Layla and shouts, "My-love-lives-in-shadows-and-dreams-when-I-wake-my-love-leaves."

When she finishes, she pretends to wipe sweat from her brow and says, "There. One sentence."

Everyone cracks up at that. Amidst the laughter, Jeremy gives his usual thumbs-up of approval, which signals the end of another filming session. I sigh loudly, feeling even more relieved than when we finished with Judith and the cheerleaders.

Wanting to leave zero time for anyone to talk to me, but especially Millie and also especially Andrea, I hop off the stage and tell Art Camp to head back to our spot in front of my cabin.

"I'm not finished drawing Andrea!" protests Shapiro.

"Maybe if you ask her nicely, you can finish your drawing later?"

She scowls a little but eventually seems to see the logic in that. Having your new favorite counselor as your babysitter evidently has its advantages.

But for once, Shapiro isn't the only, or even the loudest,

obstacle in my quest for mental peace. Terrence and Emma both plead good-naturedly to keep watching the Drama campers until lunch, while Allie asks if I can wait until she puts the finishing touches on her comic strip version of Layla. Neil doesn't ask anything, but the way he stares at his drawing book, totally absorbed in his work, tells me that probably he'd be asking to stay if he wasn't lost in sketching.

For a moment, I hesitate. It's true that I gave them an activity that can only be completed by continuing to watch the counselors. But I look at Millie, all dressed in black, laughing and chatting with her campers, and then at Andrea. The feelings I get from them intersect; I'm struck by lightning while being punched in the heart. I feel weak, helpless.

I look each of my campers in the eye. "I'm sorry, but we're going back outside."

***

The rest of the day is a miserable wrestling match between me and my guilt, and my campers suffer as a result. Once the morning is over, and we've eaten our lunch, I put them at free drawing. I make a few token efforts to answer their questions, so at least I'll seem like I am still mentally there. But it's all pretty generic advice on, like, how any drawing of a person should start with a circle and stuff. If I was one of my campers, I would feel pretty ripped off.

When they clear out for the day, a weight evaporates from my shoulders. I can't even manage my usual end-of-day banter with Shapiro. I just let her hang around silently until Aidan comes to pick her up, then offer them both a quiet, "See ya."

It's bad enough that I'm torturing myself with my conflicted feelings, but now I'm inviting my campers into my downward spiral? That's totally unacceptable, but, like all of my other tactics to shut off at least one part of my heart, knowing that doesn't seem to affect how I feel at all. I love Andrea, but I still feel... something for Millie. And I still have no desire to resolve this conflict by breaking someone's heart. So basically I'm doomed and my campers are doomed unless Madeline finds it in her heart to fire me.

But, either way, I am still doomed.

A little while after camp ends for the day, when I am sitting on the step of my cabin just pondering how terrible I am, Bailey and Jude come up to me. The fact that they're both wearing black hoodies and jeans would normally have amused me, but I am determined to sit here and be pathetic. I bite my lip, forcing back a smile.

Jude frowns and throws her hands into the front pocket of her sweater. "Your attendance at our beach bonfires has been pretty poor this summer, Mo. We miss having you around, getting all starry-eyed at every little thing. Plus, you're the only one who can rein Rory in when he starts doing campfire songs, so we kinda need you for that."

Bailey giggles and then widens her eyes. "Yes! And also you can keep him from coming on to me constantly. He's nonthreatening, but still."

The two of them, as if they'd rehearsed this, then sing together, "Moira, will you please come to our bonfire tonight? We miss you!"

I say I'll think about it.

Jude shrugs and starts walking away. That's one thing I've always loved about her. She takes my eccentricities at face value. Because she knows that prying into my peculiar little ways will lead to me asking her why she hides her spectacularly muscular, athletic body under baggy tracksuits or why she never lets me call her Judith. Our mutual understanding of our not-mutual secrets has made for a very comfy friendship.

Bailey and I don't have that kind of relationship. As

Judith heads toward the path, my other best friend stares at me with those piercing gray eyes.

I squirm a little on the step but manage a very insistent, "Bailey, I am seriously not going. Just have fun, okay? Don't worry about me."

Eventually she lets out an exasperated sigh and follows Jude. My weirdness is obviously frustrating her, but whatever. It's not like I can reasonably go. All the other times I'd turned down bonfires this summer annoyed her, but things have gotten even more complicated since then. Before, I'd just felt kind of bad; now I've escalated things to the point where it is possible that I am so much of a jerk that I don't deserve to have fun.

I stay on that step, stubborn against all comers.

Rory also tries to get me to go. I tell him I might, and also to keep his singing to himself and to leave Bailey alone while he's at it. He huffs away pretty quickly after that.

When Andrea comes over to invite me, all sweet smiles and embarrassingly visible kisses, I tell her maybe I'll see her later. She protests that she wants to get in one bonfire with me this summer. I lie and promise to be at the next one. With a confused frown, she kisses me on the forehead and walks away.

Layla and Jeremy, who are too caught up in conversation to sell me on the bonfire anyway, wisely just wave in my direction as they head down the path.

Millie, who'd been trailing them quietly, is not so smart.

She walks over to me, smiling weakly. "Hey, I think I'm gonna give this bonfire thing a try tonight. Get over my shyness a bit."

"Well, have fun."

"You're not coming down? Heard your love for these things is legendary."

I smile politely. "My friends like to exaggerate."

Millie frowns, looking shyly disappointed. "That's too

bad. I was hoping to see you down there. Guess I can't force you, huh?"

And then all of a sudden, she reaches out and touches my hand for just a second. Another shock. "You have a good night, Moira."

When she heads down the path with the others, I storm into my cabin and slam its door as hard as I can. I scream at myself, and I scream at Millie for making me have feelings for her, and I scream at Jude and Bailey and Rory for making me feel like I am a terrible friend and a terrible sister on top of already being a terrible counselor, a terrible girlfriend, and a terrible human being in general. I scream until I have no breath at all. When my lungs are finally empty, I collapse onto my bed.

My list needs revision:

"Problems I Have with Loving My Girlfriend (Andrea)"

A) Andrea's shown no sign that she feels the same. Telling her could lead to Jude-class heartbreak.

B) Millie.

C) I AM HEARTLESS AND I KNOW I NEED TO STOP THIS BUT I CAN'T BECAUSE I HATE CONFLICT AND HAVEN'T YOU BEEN PAYING ATTENTION I AM HEARTLESS.

Still, I have to admit, as I lie there languishing, heartless people probably don't feel quite so much. Probably, I'm not heartless, exactly. Probably, I am just human and selfish and miserable and stuck in a no-win scenario. Probably, I nailed it with my famous first words.

"I am conflicted," I groan as I stare at the ceiling.

Chapter Fourteen

Seeing no way out of this dilemma that doesn't involve heartbreak, self-loathing, and a meltdown that will lead to me getting fired from Lunaside, I do the only thing a sane person would do. Friday night, I turn down yet another bonfire to book a therapy session with my therapist mother.

It isn't that big of a deal, as Mom usually stays in when she can help it. Really, I think she is probably happy for the company. Dad usually has weddings and stuff to prepare for at the resort on Friday nights at this time of year, and Rory's in and out at the best of times.

To Mom's credit, she takes the whole thing very seriously. No doubt she understands that I have nowhere else to turn. She doesn't so much look the part in her loose gray sweater and jeans, but she still invites me into her office and gets me to sit in the plush, burnt-orange chair she'd chosen to make her clients comfortable. I let out a sigh as I sink into its cushions; it definitely works on me, at least.

Mom lowers herself into the wicker chair—although it looks more like a grandiose throne when occupied only by her small self—that I bought for her one Christmas. She pulls out a tiny notebook and a pencil, which seems a bit excessive. "So, Moira, you said you wanted to talk to me?"

"I did, yeah. But, uh, could you not take notes?"

My mother laughs and puts the notebook in her lap. "Yes, hmm, sorry. It's habitual."

"It's okay."

"So, what was it you wanted?"

I lean forward and sigh. "I've got a problem. I didn't know who else to ask."

She runs her hand through her short hair and looks away for a second, seemingly awkwardly flattered by that. "Um, well, I hope you're not in any trouble."

"No, it isn't that. It's just, like, I can't talk to my friends about it. Everyone's got an opinion on what I should do. I wanted objective advice. Well, semiobjective."

Mom stays quiet, nodding at what I said.

I take a deep breath and attempt to confess everything in one long exhale. "Okay, I love Andrea, but I think I like Millie too, and I hate conflict and I know I have to choose one, but I can't because someone's heart is going to get broken and mine's going to hurt either way, so I feel trapped."

There is silence after that, until Mom laughs. "Moira, honey?"

"Yeah?"

"This is a very normal conflict."

"It is?"

"At your age, of course it is. Just coming into your sexuality as you are, it's only natural to feel attraction for more than one person."

As weird as it is to be sitting here, listening to my mom academically dissect my sexuality, it's also oddly relieving to have it broken down like that. It doesn't actually solve anything, though. "Well, fine. But I'm not talking crushes here—I know that's normal. Like, I had a crush on Millie when I met her, but I'm worried that it's becoming more than that. I really like being with her, and we've held hands a few times, although I know it could have gone further. But things are getting more serious with Andrea too; I'm pretty sure I love her."

Mom presses her fingers into a pyramid that tells me she's in full-on therapist mode now. "And how do these girls, um, feel about this? Are they pressuring you to choose between them?"

I shake my head. "No? This might be just my guilty conscience."

"Hmm, well, I suppose that comes as a result of your upbringing. Certainly, we raised you to prioritize monogamy. But perhaps that doesn't reflect your current, hmm, reality?"

Raising a very suspicious eyebrow, I ask, "What do you mean?"

She coughs. "Oh, well, what I think I am saying is that one viable solution to your problem would be to redefine your relationships. If your monogamous dyad with Andrea is causing you distress, but you still have feelings for her, perhaps you could consider other, hmm, options? Perhaps your feelings for Millie are amplified by the fact that you feel you cannot have her. It might make sense to ask Andrea's permission to date her casually, and see if that makes the feelings more bearable."

I sink back in my chair and laugh, mostly at myself. I'm hung up over having fairly deep feelings for two girls, and here is my mother—who has stated that my girl-craziness keeps me from caring about life—suggesting I ask my girlfriend if we can have an open relationship. Of course, it makes so much sense.

Except it doesn't. Maybe it's possible for that to work in Mom's abstract world of research and data, but not in my world of deep feelings and not even being okay with the idea of "casual dating" because I get very attached to people. "I don't get it. One minute you're telling me I can't like girls because it means I'm holding myself back or something, and now you're telling me to date *two* girls? I'd never do that, but what's the deal?"

She grips the sides of the wicker throne and then rubs

her chin. "I'm trying to answer you objectively. And, like I said, it bothers me more that you show no initiative toward university than it does that you prefer girls. But more to the point, a growing trend seems to be that some young people are choosing to form long-term, committed polyamorous relationships. Commonly you do see groups of three, but sometimes there are even—"

"Gah, Mom! Polyamory? Who do you think I am? I'm barely comfortable with admitting I have one girlfriend."

That's when she laughs. And not her usual poor excuse for a laugh that's just a polite exhale either. This is a full-blown laugh that comes with a smile that shows her slightly crooked front teeth—teeth that have, in the past, made me feel less bad for my own crooked teeth—and makes her eyes crinkle so much that they close.

"I'm sorry," she confesses, now sounding more Mom than therapist. "I can't relate to this."

I curl up into a protective ball on the therapy chair. Of course she can't relate to this. What am I thinking? Mom is likely having an anxious fit in her head right now. I'd selfishly asked her to talk about my love life when she isn't even okay with the idea of me having a girlfriend, let alone being trapped between two girls. This must be killing her.

I let out a little whimper, resigning myself to eventually just imploding from all the distress.

Seemingly picking up on my rapid plunge into despair, she smiles kindly. "Please don't take that as censure. I was not referring to your sexuality. What I mean is that," she looks into my eyes and rests her elbows on her thighs, then says, "you certainly tax my skills as a mother."

When I wince at that, she laughs again and declares, "I'm a very sheltered person, Moira. As you know, I grew up on a farm. In my mind, every young person should want to better themselves with education. But more than that, your father's the only person I've ever dated. I can't offer you any advice based on life experience in this... particular case."

Of all the things I expected her to say, this is definitely not on the list. I uncurl myself. "Wow, really?"

She admits that she met Dad when she was twenty, at an awards ceremony for her university. She was there to pick up the award for highest overall average in her academic year, and he was there with his school, helping cater the function. The dinner was buffet-style and, when she went to get her food, Dad was there to hand her a plate and ask her how, and who, she was. Shocked but charmed, Mom invited him to sit with her. She was sitting alone anyway, since her parents didn't care about school and she technically had no friends.

That surprises me. I've always considered my mom to be very pretty in a way that I wish I could have inherited. The only thing I inherited from her is my thinness. Otherwise, she's this delicate little woman with a slight French accent who dresses fashionably and is a genius on top of that. Since I am none of those things, and am still somehow struggling with the affection of two different people, I find it very hard to believe that she'd have any trouble getting a boyfriend.

I let her know that, and she responds by suggesting that we finish this conversation in the kitchen, preferably over tea.

I agree, so we head into the kitchen, get our little ceramic teapots and our signature teas ready, and start up again. Things feel a whole lot more casual between us now that we're out here, more casual than they've been since the night Mom met Andrea, and possibly even before.

Mom takes a sip of her tea and smiles to herself. "I was never very popular, Moira. The only recognition I ever got in my life was from academic achievement, and even then it was only from professors and the like. My parents were farmers, and very traditional Acadian ones at that, so they weren't exactly happy that their oldest girl had decided to go to school, let alone at an English university. And they made sure my brothers and sisters felt the same. Family bonding just wasn't an option for me. And I've always been shy, so I just never made any close friends. Your father says it's because I'm so intimidating." She chuckles.

She explains that her reason for only ever dating Dad relates to that. She's long suspected that men don't like smart women but that they get over it if the girl is good-looking and shares a few common interests with him. As a scary-smart mousy little French girl from the back country, studying at a cosmopolitan English university, that just never materialized for her.

Hearing about her struggles, seeing as they apparently worked out, makes me oddly happy. While Mom's shyness has been staring me in the face for as long as I can remember, sometimes I forget that she wasn't always this well-respected therapist who only works out of her house because she's afraid of people. At one point, she was a shy, problem-ridden teenager too.

She'll never know what it's like to be stuck needing to decide between two possible love interests, but I will never know what it's like to be an introverted genius who had to give up her entire social network to go to school.

Still, in spite of differences like that, at our cores we are both awkward and shy women who will awkwardly and shyly work out our problems somehow, likely while downing lots of tea. The thought is strangely comforting.

It gives me very little direction on what to do about Andrea and Millie, but it's comforting nonetheless.

After a long silence, I give a little laugh—the sound of smiling out loud—and say, "Thanks, Mom."

She just smiles back.

We don't say much after that, but the ensuing silence isn't awkward. It is more the comfortable, logical result of each of us saying everything that needed to be said.

After what feels like a couple of hours of that, Mom

gets up and puts her tea stuff away, joking that it is past her bedtime. Then she comes back to the table and, to my absolute shock, gives me a hug.

At first, it's just this little shoulder-hug-from-behind affair, but I stand and let her do it properly because I want her to know this is what I've needed all along. So, we stand there and hug each other for, like, five minutes. Not a full-on squeeze, which would be awkward considering how rarely this happens. Just a normal, totally ordinary hug. And that is enough.

When Mom pulls away, she stares at me for a moment with her soft brown eyes. "I love you, Moira."

"I love you too, Mom," I cough out, my voice apparently overwhelmed by all the subdued emotion in the air.

It's the kind of moment that does not allow for extension. After only another few seconds, she gives me a nod and heads toward her bedroom, leaving me to continue sipping cups of jasmine green while the cool wind from our open window drifts over me.

As I'm making myself a second pot of tea, my brother comes through the front door and sits down at the kitchen table.

"Hey," he greets. "Jude was looking for you; I figured you'd be here."

"Judith? Why?"

He raises an eyebrow. "Uh, because best friends are weird like that and neither of us have seen you, like, at all this summer?"

I scoff. "Oh please, Judith would need a better reason than that. When she's off-island during the school year, she calls me like every three months."

Rory gives his ear a nervous scratch. "You got her pegged, don't you? Anyway, she and Bailey wanted to know why their ghostlike best friend was missing out on yet another bonfire."

"And they sent *you*?" I ask as I take my tea to the table.

"Not exactly," he replies in a low voice. "I'm kinda wondering what's up with you myself."

"Hmm?"

He stares at me and I squirm. When Rory turns his eyes on me, I can never handle it. Because our eyes are so similar, it's like peering into myself. "You've ducked out of every single bonfire this summer. What the heck's going on? You love those things more than any of us."

I shake my head. "It's stupid... It's pathetic. It's—it's—" He stays silent until I run out of disclaimers and give up with a sigh. "You wouldn't understand."

He throws up his hands in annoyance. "Of course your twin brother wouldn't understand! It's not like we have basically the same brain or anything."

"Fraternal twins aren't like that."

"Whatever. You haven't spoken to me all summer. Seriously, what's up?"

"It's really nothing," I reply with an anxious laugh. Really, I just want him to disappear so that I can keep enjoying that moment I had with Mom.

"It's not *nothing*. You've been ignoring me and everyone else! That's something, isn't it?"

I sigh and calmly set my teacup down. There is evidently no way for me to go back to enjoying a quiet evening and basking in the glow of having my mother possibly moving toward accepting me. "Hey, why don't we go outside? Maybe we'll have our own fire."

When Rory mutters his approval, we head outside to the back of our house where Dad has installed a fire pit. It's really just a pile of cement blocks and random pieces of scrap metal, but he is obscenely proud of it. Rory and I throw some wood into it, get it going with various old newspapers and skinny kindling sticks, then pull a couple of the lawn chairs that are scattered around our backyard toward it.

"It's got nothing to do with you," I explain, staring past the sharp cliff that abruptly ends our backyard, out onto the moon-speckled water. "I'm just confused, I guess."

"Yeah, and you're hiding in your Moira cave instead of dealing with your problems. That's hardly news," he scoffs.

"Yeah, well..."

He adjusts himself in his chair and matches my staring-at-the-water look. "What I don't understand is how you've got your pick of two girls when I can't even get one to so much as look at me twice."

While I'm a little surprised that my brother has so easily figured out my dilemma, what worries me is the thought that other people have also picked up on it. What if Andrea knows? What if Millie has found out I've considered choosing her, for even a second?

I cough out an, "Uh." That's literally the only reply I can manage.

Rory lets me know, in no uncertain terms, that I am being a heartless jerk no matter what I do. He explains that, in trying to avoid Millie, I'm also shutting out all of my friends who care about me more than she does.

Being a heartless jerk, I haven't considered that point.

"You need to let one of them down," he informs me. "And you've gotta do it soon. Even if you weren't turning into even more of a recluse than usual, this whole thing would still be tough to swallow. Because while you're off having your little in-head dilemmas, the rest of us have to deal with these girls. We've all gotta listen to them talking about you like you're some kind of romantic hero."

I haven't considered that point, either.

As I sit there, considering what he said, letting the breeze fill in the empty spaces in our conversation, he says, with a gravity that sounds out of place coming out of the mouth of my normally jocular brother, "Do you honestly think they don't know about each other?"

Now this point I *have* considered. I've just forced myself to ignore it because it makes me a heartless jerk among heartless jerks.

I force out another, "Uh." Once again, it is the best I can do.

He continues, "You think this is all in your head, and all you've gotta do is pick one girl, let the other one down and poof—bittersweet yet happy ending? I hate to be the one to break it to you, but they're not exactly waiting around for you to make up your mind. Millie knows you're stringing her along, but she puts up with it because she thinks she has a chance because you're afraid to so much as admit that you're with Andrea. And I suppose I don't have to tell you how your girlfriend feels knowing that you've got feelings for another girl."

"No, you don't."

I want to tip Rory's stupid chair over and throw it into the fire. How dare he? How dare he just randomly show up and ruin my perfect moment with my mother, which didn't solve anything, but felt good anyway? How *dare* he present a totally real picture of the situation I am desperately trying to avoid? I seriously want to kick him. "Well, what would you do, Mr. Doomsayer?"

"Never having *had* a girlfriend, let alone two girls who are interested in me, I really don't know for sure. I'd probably just tell Millie I couldn't be with her because I love my girlfriend, I guess."

"I can't do that!"

He sighs. "Moira, come on. Why are you so invested in being a jerk? This isn't difficult. You have a girlfriend, and as far as I know it's not an open relationship. This situation is not really something you have to monologue about."

"Huh," I reply, not bothering to tell him that his solution presents two problems. Telling Millie the truth will be hard enough, but it's not like I can just declare I love Andrea without facing a potential panic attack, either.

Suddenly, he claps his thighs and hops to his feet. "But listen, I am not going to sit around and watch you wallow. I'm going back down to the shore with everyone else. You're welcome to come."

As much as I want to retreat into my cave of tea and solitude, I have to admit that Rory is right. All of this contemplation is poisoning my relationship with Andrea, if not also turning Millie against me. It won't be long before the choice is made for me, and I end up a lonely, shy teenager—just like Mom was.

I get out of my lawn chair and grab my brother's hand, hoping to borrow courage by osmosis

"Okay, I'll go."

Chapter Fifteen

The bonfire was an anticlimax. Despite my brother's dire warnings, everyone seemed mostly happy to see me. I sat beside Andrea and she squeezed me like she usually does. And Millie wasn't glaring jealously or anything. She was just sitting there between Layla and Jeremy, being her awkward-in-crowds self.

Bailey and Judith barely noticed me at all. They had possibly been drinking, arms wrapped each other's shoulders as they were, loudly repeating, "Bonfire buddies for life!" while periodically teasing Rory for his ill-fated crush on Bailey.

Really, everything was as it should have been. Unfortunately, it wasn't enough to let me forget the urgency in what Rory had said.

I really do need to decide. And, for the sake of everyone involved, I really do need to decide *now*.

As if to emphasize the point, I'm now feeling like time is melting around me. My life has become this wash of: wake up, do Art Camp, sometimes do a webisode, have complicated feelings about Andrea and Millie, be miserable, sleep.

I watch our whole third week at Lunaside liquefy like that, which means I've officially wasted half my summer wallowing in self-pity. But as awful as it feels, it still isn't enough to push me toward the choice I know I need to make if I ever want to feel sane and normal and not sleazy again.

When our fourth week dawns, Jeremy approaches me in the cafeteria and informs me that we have three episodes left to film. They're special episodes that are intended to give in-depth looks at some of the behind-the-scenes stuff at Lunaside. Kind of like what we did with Martin and Dad, except with less exploding pancakes. He wants them to be more sober, face-to-face interview type episodes to balance out all the zaniness that came before. There's to be one with Bailey, one with both Luna and Madeline, and a final one with him.

Before I can ask how that's going to work, he explains, "See, Madeline thinks people will want to see a whole episode of me chatting about my vision, over scenes of Film Camp. Except, uh, I'm not doing that. Because nobody wants to see that. Now, don't hate me for this, but I'm putting Andrea in my place. She's a much better speaker than I am, and I'd honestly like to keep my role strictly behind-the-scenes. The world does not need to hear me say, 'Uh, I don't know' eighty-five times before I cough out something half-decently intelligent. Hope you don't mind."

Silly Jeremy, of course I mind. How can I possibly function in front of a camera, interviewing the girl I love even though I can't tell her that, all while kind of having an emotional affair with another girl?

At least it sounds like he wants to do that one last. At worst, the final episode of *The Lunaside Girl* will become some forbidden relic, forever locked away in the confines of Jeremy's camera, or wherever he stores his video files. No big loss.

"Okay, that works," I tell him with what I hope sounds like confidence.

***

That morning, we gather and find Bailey in her little backstage alcove, hunched over a sewing machine. She invites us inside with a welcoming smile, although only I can actually fit into the room with her. Once I'm inside, she gets me a chair and sits across from me.

This webisode is more my speed. The room is just a dark little box, not much bigger than a walk-in closet. There are piles of material scattered everywhere, and the air smells heavily of Bailey's own gardenia-mingled-with-coffee scent. It's really a comfy little spot; I can see why our resident costume designer rarely leaves it during work hours.

Bailey herself looks totally interview-ready too. She's wearing a purple version of the Lunaside t-shirt, low-key dark-wash jeans, and purple flats. Her hair is also fixed into a loose ponytail, making her look a bit more warm and approachable than she actually is. Harsh white light pours down on us from the room's haphazardly installed ceiling lamp, but it actually flatters Bailey's milky complexion and makes her glow radiantly.

Overall, the look of this room and the fabulously gorgeous costume designer living inside makes me feel for the first time like maybe we are producing something that will make kids want to come to Lunaside. I know I'd want to attend a camp with Bailey in it.

The two of us have a nice, relaxed chat about how she hopes to go into fashion design. She says she's been choosing outfits for her friends since first grade, and she's wanted to study it since she first learned that she could go to school for that.

Her mother was really against her going into fashion design at first, thinking that she was setting herself up to be unemployed. But, Bailey being Bailey, this only made her push herself harder to get a head start on applying. She's already gotten in touch with a top school in her field, and at least one instructor seems pretty set on working with her.

Then she talks about how she's always admired costume designers but jokes that she only really became one because her grandmother wouldn't let her come back to Lunaside otherwise. In her usual life, she draws outfits that would ideally be worn in real life. That leads her into a rant about people looking to get into the industry who only ever design for the runway.

"Like, I don't get it, do they want to be unemployable?" she asks me.

She then immediately puts her hand over her mouth, telling Jeremy he can cut that part.

We continue like that, just chatting back and forth. I think of a few nonstandard questions, which Bailey answers gracefully. I even manage to look her in the eye and say, with what I think is actually a pretty professional tone, "So Bailey, what would you say is a guiding motif in your fashion designs?"

That gets a broad, gleeful grin out of her. She squeals, "Ooh, you're after my heart with that question! My guiding motif—well, I guess it's more of a philosophy—is to make wildly creative, stunningly awesome, heart-wrenchingly beautiful clothes for real people. Not *just* for those of us built like clothes hangers, no offense to the models out there. Beautiful clothes for beautiful people, because we're all beautiful, aren't we?" She finishes with a wistful smile.

Shortly after, Jeremy gives his signature thumbs-up, and I think that says it all. Bailey totally rocked this webisode. Even if we're stuck with all the chaos that came before, we now have something that makes Lunaside look appealing to those who prefer their camps to be more than just riotous shoutfests and somewhat static progress updates from junior artists. It's the kind of thing that renews my hope in *The Lunaside Girl*, if not actually my hope in myself. But not even an award-winning starring role in hit blockbuster *Lunaside Girl: The Movie* could do that.

***

Madeline invites Jeremy and Andrea and me to her house for a barbeque after work on Wednesday so we can film the episode featuring her and Luna. At first she refuses to take her spot next to Luna in the swinging seat on her deck, arguing that the owner shouldn't have to talk. But Jeremy, flashing that baby-faced smile of his, assures her that future campers will be excited to see that the owner of Lunaside is such a vibrant, young-looking woman, instead of some stuffy old suit.

That flatters the protest out of her.

And Madeline does look pretty vibrant. She has on a bright orange, short-sleeved Hawaiian shirt, denim shorts, and orange flip-flops. Her short, silver hair is also gelled straight up, which, along with the silver studs in her ears, makes her look like exactly the kind of funky, almost-old lady any kid would want running their summer camp.

She, or possibly her granddaughter, has apparently imposed her influence on Luna's wardrobe. For one thing, the camp manager is wearing these thick-rimmed glasses; I wasn't even aware she wore glasses before. She's also evidently been forced to ditch her usual flowing robe-like attire in favor of a much more conservative look. Her long, brown hair is tied back in a smart ponytail, and she has on black, pleated pants, black sandals, and a shiny blue button-down shirt, along with a black blazer that features large blue-and-pink sequined flowers. Smart, yet eccentric—exactly the combination I think viewers will expect from Lunaside's namesake.

The interview turns out to be even easier than the one with Bailey. After fielding some standard questions, Madeline almost immediately takes charge of the conversation and talks about why she invested in the

Lunaside project in the first place. She tells the camera that since retiring from architecture, with more than enough money to last the rest of her life, she'd been looking to get into philanthropy so she wouldn't feel so bad about being old and unemployed.

She came across Luna's idea for a summer camp at a block party they were both attending. They were neighbors but hadn't really gotten to know each other until then.

"I heard that, and I guess my newfound philanthropy streak started acting up. I swooped in and started grilling her about specifics. I'd had a few glasses of wine at that point," she admits, "but I didn't regret it at any point thereafter."

She then gestures to Luna, who explains that the camp's name came about after lots of debate with Madeline.

"I really didn't like the idea of having a camp named after me," she admits. "But Madeline asserted her position as owner and refused to back down. She said, 'You've had to go through life with a name like Luna; now's the time to make use of it!'"

Madeline then explains how Lunaside became a day camp because a lot of the parents would be cottagers who'd like to see their children in the evening. The cabins were built based on her own designs, not only to recruit the best counselors, but to help these junior professionals meet likeminded people in their fields.

After that, they start getting a bit sentimental, talking about their hopes for the camp in the future, until Jeremy gives his signal and cuts them off.

With the interview out of the way, Madeline promptly fires up the barbeque and shares dinner with us on the deck. She's cooked tenderloin steaks, serving them on burger buns, for Andrea, Jeremy, Luna, and herself.

Once everyone else starts eating, she presents me with a nicely grilled corncob.

"I heard you were vegan," she says, "but I'm still figuring

out what that really means. I didn't want to see you go hungry, so I figured, 'Hey, you can't go wrong with corn.'"

I laugh and nibble at it. The slightly smoky taste of the barbeque mingles well with the almost-cloying sweetness of the corn. I'll be hungry less than an hour from now, but that's okay. We've filmed two webisodes in a row that make me feel like I'm an okay actor who can handle professional work quite nicely. That's worth more than a full stomach.

***

Madeline organizes a second barbeque for the final episode. She invites all of the counselors this time, so filming seems a bit more daunting. I try reminding myself that everyone here supports me and thinks I'm a good actor.

But I am not in any mood to be supported. This filming session is going to be awkward, and there is nothing I can do about it.

Andrea sits in Madeline's swinging seat, while Jeremy directs me to the picnic table. I obey without protest. Being this close to my girlfriend, knowing I have to appear on camera with her, makes it difficult to stand up anyway.

And she definitely isn't helping with that. She's wearing a blue-and-gray argyle sweater vest, a white button-down shirt, and freshly shined dress shoes along with her signature slacks. Her hair is gelled back for once, rather than to the side, which seemingly evaporates all those cowlicks and actually makes her look sort of dashing. Staring at her gives me this strength-sapping, warm feeling that makes me wonder if I can even get anything out of my mouth that isn't just "Andrea, I love you. What am I going to do about that?"

But I manage somehow. And with my fumbling questions, I prove to everyone why Andrea is perfect for this job and why she'd be perfect for any job remotely related to film. She talks about the storyboarding process like it's pure bliss; she discusses the decision to film the documentary the way they did so passionately that even I start wondering if I should start watching movies. Her blue eyes shine with such obvious love for her craft that I can't help but ask her more questions, just to get more enthusiastic, brilliant answers out of her.

I do that until Jeremy taps me on the shoulder and flashes a thumbs-up in my peripheral vision—presumably for the last time ever.

That gives me a little weird pang of something I can't describe, but I don't get a chance to think about it. After we wrap, Andrea invites me to sit with her on the swing seat while the rest of the counselors join us on the deck to offer their congratulations. Layla compliments my poise and delivery before scampering off to find her mother. Bailey remarks that the sundress I'm wearing cutely matches the blue in what Andrea is wearing. And Rory makes a weak joke about how he'll figure out a way to profit off his sister's newfound fame because he can never just give me a compliment.

Judith just gives my hand a firm shake and says, "You never stop amazing me, Mo. If I had half your gift for winging it, I wouldn't get into half as much trouble as I do."

"You could try not being impulsive?" I tease.

She shakes her head. "Never gonna happen."

Madeline and Luna offer their polite congratulations in tandem. Luna thinks the filming was beautiful, and Madeline hopes that my wonderful acting skills will keep her—and Lunaside—in the black for years to come.

Only Millie abstains. And from the way she's awkwardly hovering beside Layla as everyone laughs and jokes around as Madeline serves the food, it really might just be her shyness at work. I imagine it's more than that, but it seems a reasonable enough explanation that I am able to put it out of my head for a while.

Once everyone finishes eating, Madeline pulls out a large bottle of sparkling wine and asks if we are all of age. Everyone yells that they are, even though some of us aren't. Then she jokes that our contracts contain a hidden clause where we can't sue her later, if we wake up with second thoughts about drinking with our employer. When she comes around to pour a little bit of wine in the bottom of everyone's plastic champagne glasses, Andrea takes one while I hold up my hand and tell her I don't drink.

In my head I tell her, *Never in my life have I touched alcohol, and I am absolutely in no state to start tonight.*

She just blinks like I've told her I think I can fly and says, "Hmm, Luna's the same way. Different strokes, I suppose."

Once the sun sets, and our employers go inside, a bottle of apparently-not-sparkling wine also starts making the rounds, and then possibly another after that. Perhaps because of that, this celebratory-yet-sedate wrap-up barbeque slowly transforms into a relatively rowdy lawn party. Jude and Bailey, who are walking around with their arms around each other, have started singing about friendship again, while Rory makes increasingly clumsy come-ons toward Bailey and eventually also toward Jude.

That proves to be his undoing. With a disgusted yell, Judith shoves him, causing him to tumble to the ground and stay there.

Jeremy and Layla are sitting on the edge of the porch, chatting about the philosophy of directing and how Layla has to admit that he has talent even though she looks down on film people in general. He smiles placidly and responds with some only slightly slurred comment about how similar minds transcend genre or something.

As Andrea, who is still sitting with me in the swinging seat, starts groping me sloppily, I start to wish I am sitting with them. Seeing my friends drunk is a surreal experience, and not one that my never-been-to-a-party-in-my-life brain is ready to process. For a while, I sit there stunned, as if I'll catch their drunkenness by breathing the same air.

I want to shake Andrea off and, seeing how badly I need to stay on her good side right now, preferably without hurting her feelings. Do drunk people remember insults from the right before? It's annoying the way she's just sort of reaching out, touching whatever, and attempting to kiss me, but luckily her drunkenness and her shortness combine to ensure that she's mostly kissing air.

I decide to just sit there until she tires herself out, which isn't long. Soon enough she's making sleepy noises and snuggling into my lap.

She mutters something that sounds suspiciously like, "I love you, Moira," before going completely quiet.

That makes me even more uncomfortable than the drunken groping. Do those words count when drunks say them? I decide not to put much faith in them. I simply help her back into a sitting position and get off the seat, trying to forget that she said them at all.

Not wanting to leave her alone like this but also wanting to get away from her drunken self, I compromise by sitting on the edge of Madeline's deck. Since all the other partiers have moved to the lawn, it's quiet here now. And the fact that the moon is mostly out on this surprisingly warm night means I can feel a bit of my own brand of drunkenness to distract me. I swing my legs off the edge of the wooden deck, attempting to distract myself both from the anxiety I feel from this night of too much socializing and my slight irritation at being drunkenly groped by my girlfriend.

And that's when I see her, just walking along in Madeline's backyard as if she has nothing better to do than stroll around aimlessly while there is a party going on.

"Millie?" I ask, before I have a chance to think about what I'm saying.

She immediately notices me and slowly starts walking

toward my perch on the deck, her head down most of the way. With a little hop, she joins me.

"How're you doing? Enjoying the, uh, festivities?"

"Um, honestly? Seeing my entire circle of friends drunk is not something that's going down easy."

"Heh, no pun intended?"

"Exactly."

"Yeah, I don't drink, either. But I do go to parties sometimes. It can be tough."

She moves a little closer to me and puts her hand on top of mine like we're the ones who are drunk and my girlfriend isn't passed out behind us.

But maybe scenery drunk is like being regular drunk, because with a sudden rush of boldness I say, "We really shouldn't be doing this."

"I know. I feel so bad." She pulls her hand away immediately. "I've never been like that. And, like, you're the only girl I've ever felt anything for. Heh, I guess I'm off to a bad start, huh?"

"A terrible one," I assure her.

But then I look her in the eye, and all that scenery drunk boldness leaves me. The fact is, we aren't drunk. And Andrea really is still passed out behind us. There is really no sane reason for why my brain is making me think the thoughts I'm thinking at this moment. But Millie is still Millie. Same sunset voice, same perfect curves, same deep thoughts, same grassy-sandy smell, same ghost eyes.

There is a moment, a terrible moment filled with everything, where we just stare at each other. Then instinct takes hold and I move my head toward hers. Closer and closer and closer, until our lips meet.

Chapter Sixteen

I awake the next morning in my cabin. After directing Andrea to her bed, I considered going home just so I'd be guaranteed time to think, but by then it was way too late. Besides, I was totally drained. Physically drained because I don't like socializing at the best of times and because my bedtime is ten p.m., not whenever-in-the-almost-morning o'clock. Mentally drained because cheating on your girlfriend while she's passed out behind you is apparently an exhausting experience.

The really terrible part is that kissing Millie ended up being not all that great. It wasn't at all like kissing Andrea. There were no exploding rainbows; all I felt was the awareness of her tongue in my mouth. More being drenched by a bucket of yesterday's cold, used-up rainwater than being struck by lightning. Not exactly pleasant.

Thankfully, the kiss didn't last long. Within a few seconds, Millie got the hint and pulled away. Her tear-filled eyes told me that she'd gotten more out of it than I had but understood how I was feeling.

She let out a single, pathetic laugh. "Heh, guess that settles that."

I appreciate how cool she was about it, but I have to disagree. Sure, it made me realize that I only wanted her because I couldn't have her. As gorgeous, smart, and like a mirror of me as this girl is, my heart evidently only wants the little geek with no social skills. That's great, but I still made out with Millie. Who cares how I feel about it? It happened, and that's not the kind of thing relationships exactly bounce back from.

So, for the first time in a very long time, I sleep late. We don't have a clock in our cabin, and a morning cloud cover makes it tough to see where the sun is, so it's hard to tell how late. But I know it must be pretty well into the morning because of the way Bailey is lounging on her bed, with a hand resting on her cheek, watching me wake up.

"That's not creepy at all," I groan, still a bit groggy.

She smiles placidly. "Oh, be quiet. Watching you wake up is a fascinating novelty—like seeing kangaroos being born or something. How was your night?"

"Terrible," I reply without thinking.

To keep her from getting suspicious, I qualify that with, "I just don't think I was ready to see my brother, my best friends, and my girlfriend get drunk in front of me."

Bailey gives a half-smile. "Uh, well, Jude and Rory definitely were, but I was *not* drunk."

I sit up a little. "Uh, you weren't?"

She scoffs. "Of course not! All I had was a glass of wine. Do you honestly think I'd do that with my grandmother right there? She's relaxed and all, but I'm not sure she'd be above ratting me out to Mom if I got too rowdy."

"Huh," I reply, wondering what this means. Did she see anything? She and the others were on the front lawn, while Millie, Andrea, and I were on the deck. Logistically speaking, she can't have seen much. She might have seen Millie and me holding each other, but that can be explained away easily enough.

Then comes the gray-eyed stare. "Something happened last night, didn't it?"

"Huh? What are you talking about?" I ask, shuffling on my bed, as if I can literally dodge Bailey's words.

She bites her lip. "Why don't we do Miho's this morning? You can tell me all about it. Maybe we could ask Jude too."

I stare at her, not following at all. Or at least pretending not to. She's clearly figured something out, but I'm still not sure what. And until I know, I am just going to lock myself down to keep from seeping more hints out of my pores or whatever. "Judith? Why? She hates tea."

Bailey stares at the floor and laughs a little condescendingly. "I didn't want to embarrass you, but when I said I wasn't drunk, I meant it?"

I have to respect her tact. "Oh."

"And I suggested Jude because, uh, in my expert opinion, you've stepped into a two-best-friend sort of problem."

"Hmm," I reply, realizing that I'm in no position to argue. I definitely need the help.

***

Jude ends up coming after Bailey points out that it's an emergency while also lying that Miho's has started serving espresso. But she doesn't seem all that surprised when she is told they don't. Without missing a beat, she goes for their pu-erh tea, which impresses me a little because it has an odd taste not really suited to non-tea-drinkers like her. But she seems to like it. She takes a sip and jokes, "Apparently clay with fish in it is a good combination."

And with no Layla to thwart me, I get Bailey into the spirit of it too. I think she'll like this special hibiscus-chrysanthemum blend they have, because she really likes floral scents. She tries it, and she says she likes it, but that is after adding about eighty of the all-natural vegan "sweetener cubes" that Miho's provides to less-experienced tea drinkers.

Once we grab a table on the deck, Bailey takes a sip of her tea and squints at me. "Well? Last night! Details!"

I want to tell her that I only respond to full sentences, but

Jude is staring at me pretty intently too. With a defeated sigh, I admit, "I kissed Millie."

Jude frowns into her cup. "So basically you're screwed."

Bailey slaps her on the wrist. "Be nice. But, like—wow, what was that like?"

It suddenly occurs to me that I have the worst best friends in the world. "Argh, why do you need to know that?"

She raises one perfectly plucked eyebrow. "It was good, then?"

I bury my face in my hands. "Gah! I didn't say that!"

That gets her to soften her tone a little. She puts her hand gently on my shoulder and says, "Come on, we're just here to listen. You don't have to talk about it if you don't want to. But I think whether or not it was good is a pretty strong indicator of what you should be doing now. Because if it was, like, mind-blowingly fantastic, then maybe you should—"

"It wasn't anything, okay?" I snap. "It wasn't good. It wasn't bad. It just... was."

"Oh, that." Bailey nods. "Yeah, I've been there. And Millie wasn't drinking?"

"No."

She rubs her chin. "And Andrea? Does she know?"

"What? Of course not!"

"And you're sure she saw nothing?" Bailey asks, like I've committed a felony.

"Um, well, she was passed out in the seat behind us. So probably not?"

I watch two sets of eyes go wide, as my friends cover their mouths and laugh in disbelief. Once they've calmed themselves, Bailey looks at Jude and nods. "So, yeah, there is a high possibility that you are definitely screwed."

They keep teasing me, mostly because neither of them have ever done anything like this. As far as I know, Jude's never so much as kissed anyone, period. And Bailey, despite having experience with dating multiple guys at once, sees the whole "exclusive relationship" thing as sacred. That I'm also the shyest of the three of us only makes the teasing worse.

Once they get over the fact that I can't handle crowds yet somehow have the guts to kiss a girl who isn't my girlfriend with said girlfriend passed out nearby, I confess that I am pretty sure I love Andrea. Jude thinks I'm pretty stupid to only figure that out now, but she and Bailey both declare that they want to help me fix this mess in a way that keeps her from breaking up with me.

Judith tosses out the rather cavalier idea that I should just walk up to Andrea and say, "Hey, I kissed Millie. It sucked. Turns out, I'm in love with you."

Bailey, on the other hand, looks into my eyes and asks, "Does she love you back?"

I sputter that I didn't know, but that she said it while she was drunk.

She shakes her head gravely and warns, "Deep down in her subconscious it might be true, but never ever take something a drunk person says seriously. It's tempting, but you can't take that as evidence, really."

Jude submits that, in her expert opinion as Andrea's cabinmate, the way she never shuts up about me is probably evidence that she loves me. But Bailey shoots that one down too, because it's possible to talk about a person a lot and not be madly in love with them. In fact, she does a great job of shooting down all of Judith's contributions along with all of my attempts to provide evidence that Andrea does, in fact, love me.

It's frustrating, but soon enough I realize that she's just being her usually dominating self. Once Jude and I give up, a smile of inspiration crosses Bailey's lips. She has a plan. A plan that us mere mortals cannot possibly comprehend without her intervention.

After a long, confident sip of her likely sweeter-than-candy tea, she says, "If you want this to work, you are going to have to make a move. She already thinks you don't like her because you're so closed-off in public. Telling her about what you did with Millie now would be just asking her to break up with you. You've gotta do something to show that you're in this too. Something *big*."

"Big? You mean, like, kiss her in public?"

Bailey waves her hands and laughs. "You're adorably clueless sometimes. No one, probably not even Andrea, is asking you to change your opinion on PDA. I think her problem is that you act all weird when anyone notices that you're a couple. But, like, if you love her and you want to *be* a couple, you do need to get over that."

I cough anxiously, which is probably my allergy to reality flaring up. I want to stubbornly tell Bailey that she's stupid and that I don't have to get over anything. Then I picture Andrea, beaming because I'm acting like we're a couple in public, and my heart hurts.

"Fine," I reply. "What do you suggest?"

"Ask her out," she shoots back. "Like, on a real date. None of that long-walk-on-the-beach crap. That wouldn't mean anything coming from you, seeing as you practically live at the shore. It has to be something special, like— Hmm... The resort! You'd both be dressed up, and it'd be your chance to be like, 'Heck yes, I'm here with my girlfriend. I love her.' Her geeky little heart couldn't resist that!"

I flash back to Andrea's "Things I Hope to Do with My Girlfriend (Moira)" list. "Go on a Formal Date for Once" is *definitely* on it.

I look to Jude for her approval, but she shrugs. "It's a smooth plan. Bailey apparently knows how to charm a girl like she means it."

Bailey squints at that, pretending to be annoyed, while I just laugh. There's no question that this idea is better than the idle theories Jude and I concocted. The only problem that I can foresee is a simple, yet pretty major, one: I've never asked a girl out in my life.

That the girl in question is already my girlfriend does nothing to ease my mind. After all, she can still turn me down. And if she finds out about last night, she'll definitely do worse than that.

***

As soon as we get back to the camp, I lock myself in my cabin, grab my sketchbook, and do the only thing sure to relieve my nervousness. Things usually don't matter as much once I've drawn them, and I kind of need this to matter a little less.

It isn't the first time I've drawn Andrea. I like drawing her, but it is always from memory. She doesn't like when I draw her because she feels she isn't beautiful enough for art. But this time is different. I don't draw from memory. The Andrea on my page has her getting-to-be long hair gelled back, the way it was last night. And in my drawing, she's ditched the stuffy multiple-layers look for a simple black silk button-down shirt and her usual black pants. Her entire face is also fixed in a laughing grin.

Without really thinking about it, I've drawn her as I imagine she might look on our date. Assuming I summon the courage to ask her.

Seeing her like this makes me kind of excited for the possibility. It really *does* seem less imposing now that some version of her date-ready self is here on the page. All I have to do is ask her. Assuming no one has told her what I was up to at the party, she's my girlfriend. Her saying yes has to be a given.

So I get up, close my drawing book, and attempt to find her. Since it's still early, and also considering the night we just had, she is likely still asleep. But I head toward her cabin anyway, once again resolving to shake her awake if necessary.

Except she isn't in there. Jude and Bailey are; they're both sitting on Judith's bed, chatting about something. But Andrea's bed is empty.

"Any luck?" asks Jude, raising her eyebrows like she is ready to hear the good news.

I shrug. "Not yet. I thought she'd be still asleep."

"Maybe the cafeteria?" offers Bailey. "She wasn't in here when we got back, anyway."

Deciding that this is the only other logical choice, I head there. When I push through the double doors, I see Martin hanging out behind the lunch counter. Then I see Rory sitting alone at one of the cafeteria tables, still in the salmon-pink tank top and maroon shorts he wears to bed every night. But Andrea appears to be nowhere.

Rory notices me and lifts his white coffee mug toward me. "Moira! Wanna join me for breakfast? I'm lonely."

Martin's organic jasmine green isn't quite up to Miho's standards, but it's acceptable enough that I decide to oblige my brother.

"Wild night last night, huh?" he asks.

I shove him playfully, thankful that he'd at least seen nothing. "For *you*, anyway. I cannot believe you hit on Jude."

He smirks. "Hey now, if Jude hadn't flattened me the way she did, maybe Bailey wouldn't have offered to walk me home."

I slap his skinny arm. "You insufferable creep! You do realize she will never date you in a million years, right?"

He takes a gulp of his coffee. "I totally get that, but she's just so... Bailey. I get around her, and I just lose my head and practically want to marry her on the spot. She's so gorgeous and kind, and she's got that voice that's kind of high and feminine, with just a bit of roughness, and—"

In my head, I glibly suggest kissing her to see if that will kill the feeling. In reality, all I say is, "Okay, not to interrupt your creep-out-on-my-best-friend session, but have you seen Andrea this morning?"

Rory nods. "Yeah! She and Jeremy kicked me out of our cabin. They're editing those webisodes you guys shot. Jeremy told me it's top-secret stuff and gave me the boot."

"Huh. Well that solves that mystery," I say, wondering now when I can even get her alone to ask her. If she's working, there will be no getting through to her. Even if she does love me, film stuff comes first.

But I decide to try anyway, before my brain uncovers reasons how I can mess this up and I lose my nerve. "Hey, do you mind if I just go ask Andrea something? I don't want to leave you alone here, but it's important. I could go tell Bailey and Jude that you're lonely?"

He holds up his hands. "Please don't! Those two are never going to let me live down the fact that I came on to Jude. I apparently thought it was smooth to call her 'Coach' for some reason. They seem to think it's the most hilarious thing ever."

"Okay then," I respond with a smile. "Maybe I'll be back."

"I wouldn't mind that. I'll be here all morning, drinking my weight in coffee." After a second, he whispers, "I'd hit up Martin for some conversation, but, uh, he knows Dad, so I will not be sorting out the events of last night with him."

I jokingly pat my brother on the head, assuring him that I'll be back to keep him company, and then head for the boys' cabin. When I get to the door, I make sure to knock first. I want to just barge in, but Jeremy has been so polite about knocking on my door all summer that I subdue my impatience for his sake.

He slowly opens the door and greets me with a smile.

"Oh, hey, Moira, how are you doing?"

"Fine," I reply, attempting to peer over his head to see Andrea. When that fails, I say, "I was just looking for Andrea. I had something to, um, ask her. Do you think I could? I mean, I don't want to interrupt, but it's important."

He nods. "Yeah, for sure! Did you want to come in or—?"

"Um, maybe out here would be better? It's kind of, um, personal."

"Of course," he answers, heading back into his cabin and fetching Andrea. When she meets me outside, he shuts the door behind us. We sit down on the step.

Andrea stares at me, smiling. "I'm glad to see you. Now that we're into editing, I wasn't sure if I'd see you at all this weekend!"

Without saying anything, I pull her into a hug and squeeze tightly. I don't know if that's for courage or what, but it just feels like the right way to start this conversation.

"Well, hello to you too!" she says, shaking her head in surprise.

"Heh," I reply, rubbing my suddenly clammy hands against my thighs.

"Something up?"

I want to tell her that of course something is up. I want to tell her what happened last night. I want to tell her I love her. I want to clear my head of all these stupid hidden thoughts that I insist on keeping hidden because I'm horrible.

"Yes," I reply.

"Oh?" she asks, her smile becoming a bit more hesitant.

"No, it's good!" I assure her, even though a big part of it isn't.

"Okay," she says, resting her hand on my shoulder. "So, what is it?"

I stare at the grass and regret sitting on the step. This would have been so much easier if we were down on the lawn, where I could do my impression of an angry lawnmower to reduce all the anxiety I feel right now. "Um, I was thinking. Well, it was sort of Bailey's idea, but—"

Just for the sake of it, I imagine myself tearing up a huge handful of grass anyway. Maybe it helps. As I hear the satisfying *rip* in my head, I turn toward my girlfriend, look into those large blue eyes of hers, and say, "Will you go out with me?"

Her face goes blank. She looks mystified, astonished. For a moment, I think I've broken her. "Huh? What do you mean?"

"You and me. On a date? I want to take you out, maybe to the resort. I want to show you that I *do* really want to be with you. And I can't think of a better way to show that than getting dressed up and having dinner. You know how I feel about fancy clothes!"

She stares at me, wide-eyed. "Wow, uh, that's really great. Uh, just... Wow."

"Wow? Yes, okay, so does that mean—?"

She shakes her head, still staring in disbelief, as if the words coming out of her mouth are in a language she didn't know she could speak. "I'd love to, but I can't."

"You can't," I echo. It should be a question, but the words just tumble out of my mouth like vomit.

But then she grins and hugs me again. "Well, if you were thinking in the next little while, I can't! We're hoping to get the editing done over the next couple of weekends. We can't really do it during the week because of the camp, and Madeline hopes to have it all ready for the last day. Don't get me wrong; going on a real date with you is, like, a dream come true! But work comes first."

"Of course," I answer, even though I knew this would happen. I try to reassure myself that Andrea's borderline-obsessive work ethic is one of the things I love about her, but it isn't so easy now that my perfect plan has exploded.

She squeezes my shoulders. "Aw, don't worry! Actually, if you'd be up for it, I just thought of the perfect compromise!"

"Yeah?"

"I think so! Madeline told Jeremy and me that she's trying to cut a deal with your dad so that each of us would just contribute twenty dollars to have a little dinner party at the resort on the last day of camp. If that works for you, we could make it a date?"

I think I've mentally prepared myself enough so that I'm ready to appear at the resort as a couple. But to appear at the resort as a couple with the entire Lunaside staff present?

Maybe not, but what comes out of my mouth is a somewhat hesitant, "Uh, sure. Let's do that."

She smiles again, this time inviting her eyes to join the action. "Great!"

I smile back, reminding myself that I can't back down now. I've brought this on myself.

"Ah, this is going to be so fun!" she squeals, kissing me deeply out of nowhere. "But, uh, for now I'd better get back to editing. I probably won't see you a lot this weekend, but please stop in once a while! I don't think to take breaks."

"I will," I assure her, giving her a light kiss.

Even after she goes back inside, I stay on the step and let out a pathetic sigh. What have I just agreed to? Sure, I am probably fine with Judith and Bailey seeing me dressed up and teasing me about my girlfriend. And I know I can take Rory telling me I look like an alien in formal clothes, because deep down he's a twelve-year-old who can only give compliments in the form of insults.

And Dad will probably try his best to embarrass me in his affectionate way, but that's also nothing new. The rest of the staff will be too polite to really make me uncomfortable, so maybe I'm okay with them being there too.

The way I see it, there is only one little problem with

this plan. A tiny, insignificant concern that makes me sweat sticky drops of pure anxiety the more I think about it.

Millie will be there. I'm no longer worried that I'll get caught having feelings for her in front of Andrea, because those feelings have evaporated. It is now an issue of how Millie might react. I kissed her, and, while I got nothing out of it, she clearly did. I made her cry. Is she the kind of girl who can handle rejection? Is she the vindictively jealous type?

I recall her words from last night.

I've never been like that. And, like, you're the only girl I've ever felt anything for.

Assuming she means what she says, I'm possibly her first love. With a cold, fearful shiver, I realize that means she has no experience in this area; likely, even she doesn't know yet how she'll treat the girl who broke her heart.

Chapter Seventeen

Monday starts awkwardly enough. I end up going for breakfast around seven. I've gotten used to sleeping in a little since Saturday, and I am actually starting to enjoy the feeling of being a little more rested when I get out of bed. And now that we're into the slightly shorter days of August, five thirty isn't such a glorious time to be awake.

The awkward part is that I've stepped out of my early-morning solitude and apparently into Millie's. When I get into the cafeteria, she is sitting there alone, sipping a cup of coffee and nibbling on a bagel.

Some part of me wants to turn around and leave the cafeteria until she's finished so that I won't have to see her get sad at the sight of me or whatever she is going to do now. But I know that'll just make things worse. She'll see me leaving and assume I'm snubbing her or something. And I don't want that. Because even if I don't want to be with Millie, I still want to be her friend.

So I grab my usual tea and cookie, and sit with her. "Hey."

"Hi," she answers, staring intently at her bagel.

I take a sip of my tea to distract myself from looking at her. I want some indication of how she is feeling, but if she isn't going to look at me, then I'm not going to give her the wrong idea by looking first. "So, uh, do you and Layla have anything planned for these last two weeks?"

She grins a little but stares straight ahead. "Heh, I'm sure we do. Layla hasn't said anything, but she's pretty on the ball with that stuff. How about you?"

The truth is, I actually do have a plan for once. Not really wanting to dwell on how Andrea will probably react when I tell her I kissed Millie, I spent yesterday afternoon planning how to finish camp with my campers feeling that they haven't wasted their summer. I haven't been much of a counselor up until now, but there is still time.

But telling Millie all of that will probably seem weird. After what happened between us, listening to me talk about my plans to be the counselor I should have been all along is probably at the bottom of her list of fun things to do.

In the end I settle for a noncommittal, "Sort of, yeah. I guess I'll figure it out as I go."

"Heh, I'm sure you will," she answers, downing the last of her coffee and leaving the table.

***

When my group settles themselves into our usual spot on the grass, I announce, "I know it's hard to believe, but we're into our final two weeks of camp! And I was thinking that the best way for us to use this time would be to—"

"To not do free drawing?" Shapiro jokes, smiling in a way that suggests maybe she isn't really demeaning my skills as a counselor for once.

I squint at her. "What I was going to say was that we should use this time to work toward the goals you set for yourselves on the first day. That way, you'll have something to show your parents at the end!"

Shapiro eyes widen. "Oh."

"What?" I ask.

"Nothing." She shrugs. "Just surprised. I mean, that's a pretty great idea, and you didn't steal it from one of us. Good job."

I laugh off her backhanded praise and then invite the group to talk about how far they've gotten in meeting their goals.

Shapiro, of course, immediately confesses that she still has no goals. But she also admits that she already has an idea for her final project, so I'm not complaining.

The rest of the group has gotten nowhere with their goals. Emma blames her lack of a perfect specimen drawing on her family's cottage not having cockroaches. Neil claims that he is still terrible at drawing waves, although he really is improving. And Terrence still has no short comic to show for his time with me.

Allie has forgotten her goals entirely. But with a quick glance at the front of her drawing book she says, "Right! Well, I think I can at least give this thing a title. Don't know about showing everyone, though."

The first thing I do is give everyone a lesson on layouts. Layout knowledge won't really be of much use to Emma, but it will help Allie with her comic strips, Terrence with his superhero comic, maybe Neil with his waves, and possibly even Shapiro. Whatever she's doing.

Terrence and Allie really seem to like learning about layouts and ask a lot of questions, so I guide them on how to use them in their projects while everyone else works independently. Even Shapiro seems pretty absorbed by her mystery project. All morning she lays belly-down on the grass and scribbles furiously, her legs swinging in time with her pencil strokes. It makes me curious, but I refrain from asking what she's drawing, lest I pay the price for breaking her concentration.

***

Since she really got nothing out of my layout lesson,

my next target is Emma. When her mom comes to pick her up Monday evening, I let her know that I have a plan to set aside Wednesday morning for a special lesson, just for her.

She frowns at that. "Oh, I get a lot out of all your lessons, Moira. You don't need to have a special one for me. I just want to draw bugs. I'm not like Allie or Terrence. I don't need, like, fancy technical know-how. I just need, well, bugs to draw."

I squat to her eye level and smile. "But that's exactly what I meant! If you can, I'd like for you to bring a beetle for Wednesday. That way, I can do a lesson on specimen drawing, and you'll have a reference. When you're drawing something real, it's always good to have a reference."

Her frown melts. "Well, uh, yeah, I'd love that! Do you want me to bring a specific type of beetle or, uh, can I just bring, like, whatever?"

I assure her that any beetle would be fine. It's not like I can tell the difference anyway.

And so, on Wednesday morning Emma arrives to the group, grinning as she holds up a bottle that has some spindly branches and a somewhat large black bug inside.

"Ta-da, it's... a totally normal beetle." She yawns.

Emma sets her bug in the middle of our circle, and I invite our other campers to try and draw it if they want. Neil and Allie politely say that they'd rather keep working on their projects.

Shapiro only scowls at the little creature. "Ew, what is this, Bug Camp? No. Thanks."

But Terrence, at least, seems fascinated by it. He literally hops from his position in the circle and stares into the jar, following the bug's movements with his head. "Oh, sweet! I know I'm not good enough at drawing to sketch the little guy like you can, Emma, but would it be okay if I drew him into the comic I'm doing? He'd be the perfect sidekick for its main hero, Bug Girl."

"Um, sure," Emma replies, flipping open her book and making a very obvious show of being wrapped up in drawing the bug.

The beetle remains our honorary camper for the rest of the day. No one really seems to mind it being there, and I find it pretty gratifying when Emma proudly scoops him up into her arm at pickup time and says, "I think I'm on track now. I have, like, an eighth of a specimen drawing right now, but this is one drawing I am definitely going to finish."

If she really does manage to finish something this summer, I'll consider myself a success. At least where she is concerned. Although I guess Terrence and Allie are well on their way to making the most of this summer now too.

The only real dark spot on my confidence now is Neil. Shapiro is technically one too, but I know she is both going to do her own thing and somehow learn from me no matter what I say, so I'm not as worried about her.

But Neil is already a pretty decent artist, so a special technical lesson probably won't help him like it has the others. And he's a bit shy. Being singled out like that will probably make him uncomfortable anyway. Still, I know I have to do something, if only to help him feel as encouraged as a talented kid like him deserves.

***

That evening, I use my dilemma as an excuse to convince Jeremy to let me steal Andrea away from their editing for a quick dune date.

Not that we'll really be talking about it much.

The sun is already setting when we get to the dune. For once, Andrea takes off her shoes without being told, which is maybe why I kiss her even before we get to the end of the path.

When I pull away, she looks up at me and smiles. "Maybe

I should get buried in work more often."

I lead her down the path, and we sit in our usual spot. "No, I think I should just do that more often."

Her goofy grin tells me that she probably agrees, so I kiss her again. I don't go any further than that because I know she has to get back to editing. But I think I could. For once, I am just too wrapped up in enjoying our brief time together to worry about who is watching us and what they are thinking.

I put my arm around her, and feel a warm tingle as she tucks her head into my ribs. "I guess I should get to the point of why I stole you from editing, huh?"

"Oh, maybe. But Jeremy's a very talented editor, you know," she hums, lightly rubbing my leg.

"No, we really shouldn't. Don't get me wrong, I really want to! But you'll regret it later. Your geek gene will kick in, and then you'll be sad because you missed out on an evening's work for me."

She giggles. "I doubt that. But, okay, why did you steal me away? You said it was something about your camp?"

I admit that I just used my lack of ideas for what to do for Neil as an excuse to get her alone but that I really do need the help. When she asks me what my camper is like, I tell her about how he spends a lot of time on the water with his parents and how he loves drawing waves. Then I mention that he's shy and probably won't want me to do something special for him, so I'll have to be sneaky about it.

She makes a pleased little noise, something between a groan and a laugh, then pulls away from me and looks into my eyes. "It's adorable that you care so much, but I think the answer is pretty simple in this case."

"Really?" I ask.

"Well, I don't want to state the obvious, but you say this kid loves the water and is a shy artist?"

"Yeah," I reply, nodding at her so she'll reveal whatever idea has made her so happy.

"You should know what he wants better than anyone, then."

Before I can tell her I have no idea what she means, she pats me on the shoulder and says, "But maybe I should get back to editing. You've probably got another lesson to plan."

I stand up and kiss her good-bye, but I could just as easily follow her. Because I really have no idea what she's talking about, and sitting here on the dune isn't going to change that.

But then I sit back down, and it does.

Of course I know what Neil wants. If he is anything like me, I know exactly how to help him end this summer feeling like he got everything he could out of my camp.

**

By Friday morning, I get Luna's permission to take Art Camp on a field trip to my dune. Neil smiles shyly and admits that he hoped we'd do something like this, while the rest of the group tells me that they're happy for the change of scenery.

When we reach the end of the dune and find a marram-grass-free place to sit, I spread my arms, take a deep breath, and tell everyone that the dune is my favorite place in the world.

"I think it's important for artists to have special places like this," I explain, practically sparking from the excitement of sharing this place with a group of possibly like-minded people—who cares about their age—for the first time ever. "Even if you aren't into life drawing, it's useful to have a place you can go to tune out the world for a while and focus only on your art."

I then let everyone know that, while I am technically going to give a lesson on landscape drawing, they are free to work on their projects if they want. It's slightly disappointing when everyone except Neil immediately starts working on their projects. But the way he holds his notebook toward his face suggests that he is so into this activity that he wants to take notes, which makes me feel better.

And that's exactly what he does. While everyone works quietly, pausing only to comment on how nice the offshore breeze feels or how high we are from the shore, Neil scribbles on his page.

When we start packing up for lunch, he grins as he shows me a page full of point-form notes. "Uh, I know I didn't exactly, you know, draw anything. But it was informative? Don't worry, though; I'll have something by the end of next week. Thanks."

By the end of that day, I'm more confident that Art Camp is going to end successfully. Neil, Allie, Emma, and Terrence seem to be on track to meet their goals. They'll leave my camp impressing their parents and making me look like a great counselor, rather than one who was just really amazing on the first day and never again.

Shapiro's progress is still a mystery, but asking her about her project only yields a very sharp, "It's a secret!" so I resolve to leave her alone until she is finished.

***

Allie is the first to finish her project, on Monday afternoon of our final week. She decides to call her strip *Allie*, which I think is cutely fitting, and turns that title into a logo. In the first panel, she has it written in bubble letters, with the "e" ending in a flourish that looks like an even more cartoony version of her comic strip self.

When I pass her strip around for the others to see, she hugs herself nervously. But then she lets out an audible sigh when everyone—well, everyone but Shapiro, who ignores it and keeps drawing—nods approvingly and even laughs at some of the jokes.

I consider it a sign that this summer is officially a win for Allie, and possibly also for her somewhat-useful Art Camp counselor.

***

Terrence and Emma finish at about the same time just before lunch on Tuesday. Before showing anyone else, they swap books and appraise each other's work.

Emma surveys Terrence's completed comic, which has Bug Girl and the Beetle fighting Centipede Man. "The art's really good but, um, cockroaches do *not* travel in swarms. They have some social characteristics, but—Oh." She stops herself and delicately runs her fingers over the page. "It does look awesome."

Terrence is a bit less critical of Emma's work. He just comments, "Wow, Emma, you're an amazing artist," and then hands it over to me.

I have to agree with him. For one thing, this drawing is actually finished. Although even if it wasn't, I would still admit that it's a pretty competent drawing of a beetle. Everything is in proper proportion and is shaded properly. She's even labeled all of the parts and written their functions. That includes the wings, which are tagged "for flying."

I smile at the page. "I know you're disappointed that it's not a cockroach. But I think you captured the beetle very well. Also, now I know what wings do!" I joke as I hand the book back to her.

She grins. "Hey, some bugs don't use their wings for flight! It's good information to have."

I assure her that it is, and that I'll remember it. Who knows when knowing which bugs are winged and flightless could be useful?

***

Neil hands me his drawing book as the parents are arriving Thursday evening, which cuts it close enough that I start to get worried. But I resist the urge to crush him into a triumphant hug when he shyly presents his drawing to me.

What I see on the page makes me a little breathless. On the horizon, he's drawn the empty shore, even including a few rocks and seashells. And he has certainly gotten better at drawing waves. He chose to draw the calm surface of the sea from the day we visited the dune, with the occasional mark of detail to depict a slight ripple.

Then there's the dune. He depicts the marram grass blowing lazily to the left, with at least an attempt to shade it so that it appears to be shimmering romantically in the sun. And the path itself appears deep with pale sand, an untouched and inviting walkway to the shore below.

"Wow, Neil, this is beautiful," I blurt. "You've really learned the trick to drawing waves. Drawing them in motion is impossible, but if you focus on one position in your mind's eye, you can usually get something down. It's not an easy skill to learn, either. I'm impressed."

"Wow, uh, thanks. So much," he replies, staring at the ground.

I insist that I am serious, with a wide smile that comes from knowing I was a good enough counselor to get four of my campers to reach their goals before the deadline.

Still, Shapiro isn't finished yet, which is actually starting to bother me. Sure, she's unpredictable and hard—well, impossible—to please, but she is still my camper. I'm not sure I can let her go home with no finished project and not feel a little sad that I've let her down.

But when she leaves Thursday evening, even though she gives no sense that she is anywhere close to finishing, I remain optimistic. She is probably just taking so long to be difficult. And for that whole evening I am confident of that.

This is Shapiro, after all. She still has a whole day to show me whatever confusing, awkward drawing she's come up with this time.

Or not.

Friday morning gets eaten up by a surprise presentation. Drama Camp sends Millie, of all people, to let our camp know that there is a big end-of-camp event going on in the cafeteria. We share an awkward smile. Then I thank her, and she quickly disappears back into the cafeteria.

My stomach sinks as soon as we get into the building. The room is mostly dark, and the words *The Lunaside Girl* are fading onto the big projector screen on the stage.

But then some jangly indie pop song with horns and tambourines unexpectedly starts playing, and I relax.

In what has to be an act of mercy, Madeline or Jeremy or maybe Andrea put together a musical montage of key moments from the webisodes instead of showing the episodes like I'd feared. There is the bit with the exploding pancake, Emma's bug drawings, Jude's psychotic training, and of course the cheerleaders. There are shots of candid stuff like Dad making a goofy face, Bailey in her costume cave with a pleased smile, Layla jumping around, and lots of other great scenes that really don't involve me at all.

The whole thing ends with a scene of me walking around Lunaside alone apparently near dawn, judging by the orange glow on everything. I make a mental note to harass Jeremy or Andrea about filming people without their permission, but it does make a nice coda.

When the song fades out and the credits roll, the campers and staff jump to their feet and cheer.

I stay sitting until Shapiro rolls her eyes at me. "Moira, stand up! You were a good actor; people liked what you did. Suck it up."

So I suck it up and stand. Really, I have to admit *The Lunaside Girl*, now that it's finished, looks like something that people might someday want to see. But maybe that's because I'm just high on feeling like I've been a pretty decent counselor in the end.

The parents apparently think so anyway. Allie, Terrence, and Emma's parents all thank me for a wonderful summer and assure me that they'll try to come back next year. Emma's mom also shows up in a cockroach shirt that she bought online, telling her that a matching one waits for Emma in their car, which ensures that she doesn't stick around for an emotional good-bye. Or anything more than a quick, "See ya!"

Saying good-bye to Neil is a bit harder. When his father comes to pick him up, I regret complimenting his final drawing so profusely. All it means now is that seeing him off will be more emotional.

When he gives me a shy little hug and says, "Thanks so much for your help this summer, Moira. I think my drawing is a lot better now," something creeps into my throat.

"Aw," I choke, "you're welcome."

I want to say something profound, like how he has talent and should keep drawing, but that's all I can manage without crying at the sudden realization that camp is really over for another year.

When those two leave, I stare at my last remaining camper. She's belly-down on the grass, still drawing frantically.

Now that Aidan Hanley—who I probably don't have to impress at this point—is the only parent left to arrive, I sit down beside her, cross my legs, and close my eyes. Just as I am on the verge of scenery drunkenness, I feel the distinct *thud* of a drawing book being dropped onto my lap.

"It's done," she declares. "You can look at it."

I hesitate to take the book. Her drawings this summer have taken my brain to some pretty dangerous places. That mirror-girl thing almost convinced me that I was in love with Millie, while that "true love" drawing almost forced me out of love with Andrea. What other life dominoes can she accidentally topple with her ill-proportioned drawings?

None, it seems. The drawing in front of me is entirely different from the ones before it. It isn't perfect by any means, but in it I see the real beginnings of artistic ability missing from her other stuff. She's drawn a girl yet again, but this one lacks the primitive look of the others. It still doesn't look like a real person exactly, but it comes closer.

This girl is wearing a sundress. The ivy one again. This time, every leaf of ivy is achingly detailed and shaded— looking better than the dress' real-life counterpart in that way. The drawing's hair is long and curly, and there's even been some attempt to shade it so that it looks shiny. Her arms and legs look stiff and the fingers and toes don't look real, but they at least remain well within the limits of the page. All fairly competent stuff.

But it is the face that makes me feel a little rush of pride. She clearly tried to make it look alive, more than with the other parts of her sketch, and it somewhat works. Her sketch girl is grinning hugely, making her eyes closed-off little lines. I suspect that she drew it like that to get out of drawing eyes, but the girl still looks joyful and entirely at peace.

Basically she looks like me at my best, as drawn by an eleven-year-old with a bit of artistic talent.

Somehow, that makes me grin. "You drew me again. And you kept it on the page."

She smiles shyly. "I love drawing you. You're not pretty or all that great at being a counselor, but you're interesting. You're quirky, and I like your sundresses and Andrea."

I chuckle. "Well, I don't *own* Andrea."

As if to debate that point, Andrea comes up behind me and wraps her arm around me. "Hey, you two. Aidan's still not here?"

She shakes her head. "No, but we've got a movie night

planned, so it's not like he forgot me."

Andrea plops onto the ground beside Shapiro. "That's cool. But you should call him and tell him to pick up the pace, 'cause *we've* got a date tonight!"

Shapiro dutifully offers to do that, but Andrea laughs and tells her it's fine.

It's around four thirty when Aidan shows up. He thrusts his hands into the pockets of his khakis and greets us with a friendly smile. "Sorry I'm a bit late."

"They have a date tonight, Dad," Shapiro huffs. "They don't want to listen to you waste time apologizing."

He looks at his daughter and then winks at us. "Oh, of course! Celebrating another successful year, huh? Well, you girls enjoy yourselves; you've earned it!"

When he starts walking back to his car, Shapiro hesitates and looks at us before shaking her head and saying, "No, I'll say good-bye to you when you babysit with Andrea some night."

"That's for the best," I reply, with a laugh at both how impossibly sad I would be not to see Shapiro again and how crazy I am for feeling that way.

When the Hanleys speed off in Aidan's convertible, Andrea puts her arm around me and says, "Bailey and Jude are waiting at your house already. The plan is for all of us to meet at the resort at seven. I know that's pushing it, but I think we'll make it."

"Huh? What?" I ask, suddenly stunned. That sounds a lot more complicated than the "wear something nice, have dinner with Andrea" plan I have in my head.

"Um, well, everyone was kind of just running around discombobulated about tonight. I might have micromanaged, just a little?" she says, wincing.

I raise an eyebrow. "How much?"

More than "just a little," it seems. She mapped out the whole evening during lunch. Millie and Layla are going to get ready at Madeline's house, which is totally fine with me. The boys will be getting ready at Andrea's place because, after her mother joins Aidan and Shapiro's movie night, she'll have the place to herself and doesn't want to get ready alone.

It was Bailey's suggestion for Andrea to take the boys to her place. She has some kind of surprise for me and doesn't want it ruined by Rory's awkward flirting.

I ask Andrea what the surprise is, but all she does is kiss me on the forehead and say, "I know this isn't exactly ideal for our first real date, but I think it'll work. For now, though, I'm going to have to go. Mom left the car at the resort and the boys are already there, so I'll literally have to run!"

She then looks me in the eye and adds in a low voice, "But I'm really looking forward to seeing you later."

I smile, watching her sprint down the path before starting for home. As I hit the sandy path, taking off my sandals as I do so, I have to admit that I'm not really sure if I feel anything about tonight. There is just too much, too many ways to feel.

There's Bailey's mysterious surprise, which should make me excited. But then there is also the fact that tonight is supposed to be the night I admit things to Andrea. Things that will probably make me lose her.

I decide to focus on the surprise for now. After all, Bailey is kind of a dominating person. Maybe she's thought ahead; maybe she's found me a cure for all the heartbreak that will ensue before the night is over.

Chapter Eighteen

Bailey is waiting for me in my room, along with Jude and, surprisingly, my mother. Mom is leaning against my closet, her arms folded so tightly that she's basically hugging herself. Judith is sitting on the floor, leaning against my bed. Bailey, meanwhile, is on the bed, holding an opaque white bag that reaches down to the floor. She's grinning a very un-Bailey grin of pure glee.

"So, um, what's in the bag?" I ask as I sit beside her.

She immediately sets it into my lap, patting it like a well-loved puppy. "It's yours."

"Mine?" I ask.

The grin returns. "Go try it on."

I look at Mom for some hint that'll give away the surprise. In return, I get a warm smile that means basically nothing. And Jude is entirely blank-faced, which tells me that Bailey has instructed her to lock this secret down. Deciding that our time is pretty limited already, I give up and head for Rory's room—the only other room with a full-length mirror.

I drop onto his bed and unzip the bag, then pull out what I find. As I suspect, it's a dress. As I didn't suspect, it looks like something I might wear.

It is a white, sleeveless dress that tapers at the waist and flares out a little at the hem, which probably will rest at about my ankles. On its own, it might look pretty plain, but it's livened up by the splashes of red, yellow, and blue paint—I assume it's paint because I can literally feel the blobs of color, raised up from the fabric as they are—placed on the right shoulder, the left leg, and diagonally across the waist.

With some hesitation, I try it on. It fits suspiciously well. Bailey has never attacked me with a measuring tape; how can she possibly know my exact measurements? But, as I stare at myself in Rory's mirror, I'm not complaining. My friend somehow found me a dress that's formal and still totally me. Without bothering to zipper the back of it, I march back into my room.

"Bailey, where'd you find this? It's beautiful. Thank you!"

My friend looks significantly at Mom and Jude. "Uh, well?"

"That's a Bailey Jarre original," declares Jude.

"You're kidding!" I exclaim, studying Bailey's face. She laughs and looks away. "You seriously made this?"

She nods. "It's based on a design I included in my application portfolio for design school. More of what I was saying about my need to make high fashion meet real life. It was probably inspired by you, anyway, and I knew you'd have nothing appropriate for tonight. I had some extra fabric in the costume room, so I just decided to go for it."

"Wow," I reply, stunned. "You're amazing! And, like, it fits perfectly. How did you know?"

She grins and pulls her shoulders inward. "Uh, lots of practice, maybe?"

I shake my head. "I don't know if practice really accounts for that, though. Like, I'm not exactly your standard model. Are you sure you're not just a genius?"

"Um, Moira? You're a giant *and* a stick. You might dress like a hippie, but you're at least the standard *build* for a model." She shrugs. "I just thought it'd be good experience, and I'm kind of psyched to have someone actually wearing one of my designs."

Then she claps her hands together. "But enough about me! We've still got a bunch of things to do before we head out! Moira, please sit on the bed."

"What? Why?"

She rummages through her bag and produces a large, flat, black box. "This is why."

"Wait, that's—"

Bailey smiles mischievously as she opens it. Inside are tiny squares of various colors, some equally tiny brushes, and a mirror. It looks a little bit like an artist's case, except evil. "Yes, it's exactly what you think. I got Grandma to go to the mainland just so you could have some vegan, organic, not-tested-on-animals makeup for your first date. Well, that, and I never get a chance to play with this stuff on other people. My other friends are all too conceited to let me do anything to their faces, and my sister never lets me make her over because she's a big geek. But with you, I've got an excuse!"

"Oh, great."

"Hush! If it helps, try not to think of it as you being made up to look like someone you're not. Think of it as one of your best friends thinks you're very pretty and is excited to make you look even more dazzling for your first date."

Her flattery works. "Argh, fine. But *minimal* makeup, please. No glam."

"Uh, don't worry. You are so totally not glam," she points out with a snicker. "Seriously, though, I'll be gentle. Just relax."

And so, for approximately the next hour, I sit still on my bed as Bailey does unseen things to my face while ominously whispering to herself. When she finally steps back with a happy little gasp at her work, I ask, "Are you finished?"

"You tell me." She smiles, thrusting the makeup box, and

its small mirror, onto my lap.

"Huh," I mutter, breathing a little sigh of relief.

I'm not sold on makeup as a day-to-day thing, but I look enough like myself that I can stand it for one night. All Bailey seems to have done is apply a layer of foundation that mutes my freckles a little and add a few small touches of color here and there. A bit of greenish eye shadow that perks up my sad-looking eyes a little, some pinkish lip gloss—nothing too drastic.

After she closes the box again, she sets it aside and gives me a hug. "Aw, you look beautiful."

At that, Jude stands up and surveys me up and down. "Mm, you do clean up nice, Mo."

Pleased that my friends care about me, but wanting them to stop being annoying, I look at them and ask, "Uh, thanks for your support, girls, but don't you have to get ready too?"

Bailey shoots Mom an odd smile and then says, "Well, we do. But this isn't *our* first date. We wanted to make sure you were put together first."

"Yeah, plus me and Bailey have had like a million dates together by now. All those bonfires, you know. We don't have to impress each other these days," Jude jokes.

Bailey glares at her. "Come along, Judith," she groans. "Let's give Moira and Phil their mother-daughter first-date moment."

"Okay, but you are not putting any of that stuff on me," she warns, pointing a finger at Bailey.

"Don't worry; I value my health too much to try." She laughs as they leave the room.

When they're gone, Mom quietly sits beside me on the bed. She finally uncrosses her arms. "You look beautiful, Moira."

"Thanks, Mom."

She spends a bit of time just staring at me and smiling. But when that starts to get awkward, she excuses herself and leaves the room. Once she's gone, I flop back onto my bed. The worst of the night is probably yet to come, but I survived the first major obstacle. I've been made presentable and am not having an anxious fit over it. That's impressive, I have to admit.

Mom returns a few minutes later with a long, slim, pink box. Before I get a chance to ask her what it is, she bustles over to my closet and starts rooting through it. When she reemerges, she is holding a pair of white wicker flats.

"These should do nicely." She drops them at my feet. "Try them on."

I stare at the shoes, not having considered footwear until this second.

Seemingly having read my mind, Mom gives a long sigh. "Moira, you cannot wear those beat-up old sandals to your date."

Grumbling at the fact that she's probably right, I stand and put them on. They fit well enough, although they cut the back of my feet with their never-worn stiffness. Mom bought them back in June, thinking they'd be perfect on the off chance I somehow happen to have a massive change of heart and actually decide to attend my prom next year.

"They fit," I declare, dropping back onto the bed.

"Excellent," she says, sitting down beside me.

"I guess so."

She stares at my closet door. "Um, I suppose you could— it's just more of what I was saying about life scripts, but open the box."

Obediently lifting its lid, I see a pair of clear drop earrings and a matching pendant. They seem to be made of regular glass and look pretty unremarkable. But I don't want to disappoint Mom, so I utter a quick thank-you.

She runs a hand through her hair and sighs. Then she picks up the pendant, fastens it to my neck, and runs the wire backs of the earrings through my ears with loving precision.

When she's finished, she smiles weakly and tells me I can take them off again if I want.

I tell her I'll keep them on, as what little scraps of jewelry I own are handmade and even less formal than what she's offering.

With that assurance, she starts rambling about life scripts again before admitting that she bought the earrings and the pendant as a set at a pharmacy, about twenty-five years ago. She was twenty at the time and had neither the time nor the money for fancy jewelry, starving-yet-star student that she was.

She laughs to herself. "This sort of thing is what I mean by life scripting. Just silly little events that all parents hold for their children, whether we like it or not. I guess when I met Andrea I worried that life would somehow be different for you and felt I had to grieve... something. Of course, I know better now. I suppose, in spite of what I've read and researched, I just haven't lived as much as I could have."

"That jewelry is what I wore to my first date with your father," she explains. "Even then, I was sentimental in spite of my education. Sometime after Ewan and I had gotten serious, I put those things away, saving them for the future daughter I hoped to have. I was scripting your life before you were even considered!" she exclaims, throwing up her hands.

I press the pendant between my thumb and my forefinger, feeling its smooth, cool surface with new appreciation.

She smiles. An eye-crinkling smile that makes the tiny lines around her eyes more obvious, but she doesn't look happy, exactly. Her brown eyes look watery and maybe wistful. Is she sad that I am going on this date with Andrea, the one who is difficult, instead of Millie, the one she likes? Does it depress her that giving away her first-date jewelry to her seventeen-year-old daughter makes her feel sort of old? Is she really just happy for me?

I decide to go with the last one. "Th-thanks, Mom," I

utter, this time with total sincerity.

She nods firmly. Then she looks away for a moment and casually brushes the back of her hand across her face, sniffles, and faces me again with a quiet laugh. "I just want you to know that, in spite of what I might have said, I'm very proud of you, Moira."

Not wanting to cry, lest I mess up Bailey's makeup job, I pull my mother into a warm and conveniently silencing hug. She, having no such makeup-based restrictions, lets out a few sobs as she squeezes me back.

Once she lets me go, she holds me at shoulder's length and smiles, her eyes still watery. "Have a wonderful night."

"Thanks, Mom. I will," I reply, not so sure that I'm telling the truth.

Regaining her composure with a quick clearing of her throat, she says, "Well! I'm going to go have a cup of tea. And you, I think, should probably go find your friends."

I chuckle. "Maybe."

But it turns out that I don't have to go far. As soon as Mom heads into the kitchen, Bailey and Jude come back into my room, ready to go.

Bailey is wearing a simple, black, knee-length, sleeveless dress, a silver bangle on her left arm with earrings to match, muted makeup, and wine-colored lipstick. She's also piled her long hair high atop her head in some kind of elaborate style that leaves two strands cascading enticingly down the sides of her narrow face. She looks absolutely stunning, but that doesn't surprise me at all.

The real triumph is Jude, who hates formal wear about as much as I do. She's put a bit of gel in her almost-black, close-cropped hair, spiking it upward. Otherwise, she's wearing a strikingly pink, collared shirt, along with a black vest, jacket, and pants.

Since I know Bailey would just shrug off any compliment I sent her way, I ignore her and squint at Jude. "Is that—Is that you, Jude? What—what are you wearing? That doesn't look like any tracksuit I've ever seen."

"Hey, shut up!" she shoots back. "Oh, and I'm not a *total* sellout," she declares, rolling up one of her pant legs to reveal a fairly expensive-looking pair of black running shoes.

"I'd expect nothing less," I laugh. "But I think you look great."

"Yeah, well," she answers, shuffling anxiously, apparently inheriting Bailey's inability to take a compliment. "We ready to go yet? I'm getting fidgety and also hungry."

Seeing no reason to sit around, I tell her that we can probably just go now.

***

When we get to the resort, only Andrea is waiting outside. She informs us that the boys have already gone inside to join the others. Taking a hint that may or may not have been there, my friends look at each other.

Bailey says they better get inside too.

Once we're alone, I pull Andrea close. "Hey there."

"Hi!" she chirps.

She's wearing a shiny, purple button-down shirt, her usual pleated slacks, and freshly shined dress shoes. And her hair is once again styled in that dashingly careless-looking, combed-back style she had the evening of our interview.

She doesn't look exactly like my earlier drawing, but close enough.

Overwhelmed by a sudden instinct to kiss her all over, I move in close and squeeze her butt for a split second. When her eyes go wide with surprise, I kiss her more passionately than I ever have in such an open space. Because it doesn't seem to matter all that much now if some bored retiree decides to gawk at us. I know what this night is going to bring. There's a good chance I will never kiss Andrea again after this moment.

***

When we get inside, everyone except Madeline is already seated. She's standing with her glass raised, apparently in the middle of a toast.

As we enter, she cheers, "And let's hear it for our Lunaside Girl! May she keep Lunaside financially viable for many years to come!"

Everyone applauds.

I smile bashfully, and quickly sit down with Andrea across from me.

We just sit there quietly staring at each other because it's far too loud for conversation. Madeline keeps toasting people—Luna, Jeremy, Andrea, the counselors, the campers, Dad, and Martin, who'd heroically turned down the offer of dinner to help Dad prepare the food—until Jeremy suggests that we give Madeline a toast. Everyone taps the table riotously at that, causing the head of Lunaside to smile warmly and finally sit down.

Our food arrives soon after. Dad hand delivers a few of the plates—mine, Andrea's, Rory's, and Madeline's—and bellows at his staff to do the rest.

He evidently decides that I'm having Pasta Moira for dinner. That's fine because I think it's the only vegan option on the menu, anyway. He bestows upon Andrea some kind of tiny steak with a blob of something orange on top. She pokes at it inquisitively.

Once we're served, most of the chatter dies as everyone enthusiastically begins their meal. There are a few comments on how good the food is, but that's all. Even Andrea and I, although we stare at each other frequently, keep quiet. She is no doubt a bit entranced by whatever Dad has added to her steak, while I am dreading what is to come.

As the evening goes on and our dinner plates are eventually exchanged with dessert—I go for the muesli cookie, and Andrea opts for Mousse Cake a la Philoméne—I start to feel like maybe I'll just let the evening pass letting Andrea know neither how I feel about her nor what I did with Millie.

After all, the plan is to tell her everything on a date. This isn't exactly a date. There will be other dates—real ones. Other opportunities to break her heart and mine.

I anxiously pick at my cookie. Of course I'll have to tell her everything. It is in my best interest to tell her I love her, and telling her about Millie is the right thing to do.

But I can't just blurt it out here. And waiting until the end of dinner, when all of us leave as a group, will be just as impossible. Once this thing ends, we'll possibly be trapped by our fellow counselors into chatting all night about the camp. After that, I'll be too tired to say anything coherent.

With a deep breath, I lean forward and ask her if she wants to go outside. When she smiles quizzically in response, I tell her I have something important to say. I stand, suddenly feeling very mature, and wait for Andrea to make her way around the table.

I scan our group, basking in everyone's end-of-summer cheer. Rory is telling Jeremy how he thinks he is a talented filmmaker, while Madeline tells Luna that these things always make her sentimental. I watch Luna open her mouth, possibly to let the camp owner know that she'd be less emotional if she'd stop at one glass of wine, but I don't hear what she's saying. I'm staring at the single-seat gap in our table, the half-eaten desserts, the carelessly pulled out chair, and the empty booth.

A sudden, cold wave of dread washes over me. Layla and Millie left at some point, and I didn't even notice. What if they are still outside? How can I possibly tell Andrea anything with Millie there?

With a bit less confidence, I take Andrea's hand and lead her out of the resort.

The gravel of the parking lot reflects the perfectly moonlit night, giving it an eerie bluish whiteness. I stare at it for a while, just letting the reliable offshore breeze engulf me. Then I take Andrea's hands, look into her eyes, and steady myself with a quick cough.

"Andrea, there's something I need to—"

My speech is shattered by the unmistakable sound of someone's sobbing.

I turn around and see Millie. She is sitting on one of the greenish wooden blocks that marks the edges of the parking lot. Layla is there too, her arm wrapped around her.

Millie is wearing this black band-jacket-looking blazer tonight, along with silvery-gray dress pants, a similarly colored button-down shirt, and silver flats instead of those black flip-flops. Her matching jewelry—stud earrings, a couple of rings, and a simple silver chain necklace—shines in the moonlight.

Even though seeing her now doesn't provoke the same reaction it did before I kissed her, there is no denying that she's still the most striking girl I've ever seen. Seeing her generally sleepy-looking face twisted with crying, those whitish eyes filled with tears, gives me a weird feeling in my stomach.

Can a person vomit with guilt? Because I am about to.

Directing my girlfriend's attention away from the girl who is very likely crying because of me, I repeat, "Andrea, there's something I really need to tell you."

With a concerned glance at Millie, I add, "And I don't think you're going to like it."

Chapter Nineteen

Propelled by the fuel of all the times I've screwed up, the words fly of my mouth.

"Andrea," I say, letting my tongue savor each syllable because I know it'll be the last time I get to say her name lovingly, "I kissed Millie."

There comes an unearthly silence after I say that. It's like the whole world stops making noise, just to take in the enormity of what I've confessed. Millie stops crying; the wind stops blowing. Even the rocks seem quieter, as stupid as that sounds.

Andrea is no exception. She drops my hands and goes so silent that the only hint I have that she's still breathing is that she's still standing.

A few mute seconds, and the world's volume returns to normal. Millie starts crying again, but weaker now; the breeze picks up. And the rocks get loud again, however that works.

Only Andrea remains noiseless. She scowls at me, her eyes set to overflow. I want her to explode suddenly, to kiss me off in a spectacular pyrotechnic display of all the hatred at all my little neuroses and anxieties that have been building these past five months. I don't just want my heart broken. I want it obliterated with dynamite; I want the pieces carried off on the wind and discarded in the ocean. Because that's what I deserve.

Except, she doesn't do that. She also doesn't wind up and punch me in the face like some kind of enraged Judith.

To my horror, she doesn't do anything. She simply blinks away her tears and starts walking away, then running, in the direction of Lunaside.

Without thinking, I take off after her. How can I possibly know what her plan is now? She's given me nothing to go on. What if she's decided that tonight is a good night to plummet off one of those dangerously rocky cliffs past Lunaside? The thought makes me angry. How can she just leave? She's had no trouble at all being open about our relationship. So why can't she be equally shameless about being angry with me?

When I reach the camp and see Andrea running across the Lunaside field, I notice in my peripheral vision two figures jogging behind me. Normally having people see me talk to Andrea like she's my girlfriend makes me anxious, but now that she's about to dump me I don't care at all.

The sad irony of that isn't lost on me.

I find Andrea sitting on her step. She's hunched over with her arms folded. She looks even smaller than usual, like a hurt and lost child. With hesitant steps, I attempt to join her, or get her to come over to me. Just something to give me some chance at making the other confession that I'd actually intended to make first.

Evidently, that is a terrible idea.

Even before I reach the step, Andrea growls, "Go. Away."

I raise my hands as if to defend myself. "Andrea, please listen! That's not the part I meant to say first. What I meant to say was—"

"I don't care. Go away."

"There's more to it than just that," I say, realizing about halfway through my sentence that I'm pleading. "You don't understand!"

That gets her off the step. She marches toward me,

glaring, then screams, "Of course not! I'm just silly, naïve, little Andrea Grey—fun for a while, but too childish and embarrassing to be with once a real adult came along. Of course *I* wouldn't notice my first-ever girlfriend slowly slipping away from me over a couple of weeks because she's met some older girl who's smarter, deeper, better-looking, and just overall superior to me in every way!"

I grit my teeth in frustration. Sure, I probably shouldn't have said that I kissed Millie before telling Andrea I love her. But can't she be a little bit more reasonable? "I never said you were stupid. Although you are being pretty dumb right now."

"Am I?" she yells.

"The way you're not listening to anything I'm saying? Yeah, kinda."

Andrea shamelessly wipes her tears with her shirtsleeve. "I'm sorry if my politeness isn't up to my usual standards, but I really don't want to hear the rest of the story."

"Well, I think you should," I urge.

She gives an exhausted, impotent little shrug. "You might think I can't read between the lines, but this time I can. You've wanted to get with Millie all summer. Eventually it got to be too much, so you crossed the line, and now you're breaking up with me. Thanks for letting me know the reason, I guess."

"Andrea—"

The sudden sight of her tiny palm, pointed in my direction, silences me. "C-can we just not talk anymore?" She takes a deep breath. "You really hurt me," she whispers, staring at the ground. "Maybe we can talk about this tomorrow or something, but right now I think I just need to rest."

I sigh. "If you'd just let me—"

She laughs, seemingly at herself, so hard that her shoulders shake. "You know how excited I was for tonight, our first 'date'? I literally counted the days. I dreamed about it. I thought you were finally coming out of your shell, like maybe I was wrong when I thought you were just biding your time with me. I even started to think that maybe you were doing it all just because you secretly loved me, but were too shy to say it."

Now I'm the one screaming. "You idiot! I *do* love you! That was the whole stupid point of this stupid conversation!"

If there existed a laughter equivalent to being spat on, I've just discovered it in Andrea's derisive chuckle. "Why are you saying this?"

"Because I love you, stupid! Why else?"

But she just shakes her head. "I'm not sure how it works inside your bubble, but here in the real world, we don't show our love by kissing other people."

I lower my head and admit defeat. She's right. Telling her I love her can't just fix everything. It was pretty naïve of me to think otherwise.

She starts walking back to her cabin, and I don't even bother to follow. Not that I can really move, my legs wasted and wobbly from anger and guilt as they are. I want to stop her, get her to see my perspective—forgive me, at the very least. But I just watch her walk away, because telling her I love her isn't good enough, and I have nothing left.

When she stops about halfway back to her cabin, I start to wonder if: A) she's suddenly forgiven me, or B) my newfound time-stopping psychic powers have frozen her there.

It registers a second or so later that she's stopped because someone has called out to her and is now walking toward her.

For some unfathomable reason, Millie is slowly heading toward my by-now likely ex-girlfriend. She puts her hand on Andrea's shoulder as she stops.

"Listen to her," Millie says, her voice still hoarse from

crying.

Andrea throws the offending arm off her shoulder. "I told her she could have you, so you can stop crying. Just go into your cabin and have your happy ending, okay?"

Millie slaps her forehead, which seems oddly inappropriate for the situation. "Look, Moira loves you—"

"I'm sorry, what? She loves both of us? I don't know about you, but I've got too much self-respect to care."

I watch Millie clench her fists. "You don't have to listen to me. I'm only telling you this because I care about Moira, and I'd hate to think that I messed things up for her."

When a few seconds of silence make it clear that Andrea is not getting it, Millie takes an audible breath through her teeth and says, "Sure, she kissed me. But I knew right away that wasn't what she wanted, even though I'd personally been waiting for it all summer—not that I expected it to happen. She figured it out just after that. Heh, you wanna talk heartbreak?"

She does not stick around to explain why she was crying outside the resort. Layla, who's sort of been skulking in the shadows during all this, wraps her arm around her friend and leads her into their cabin.

Andrea stands perfectly still, seemingly petrified by Millie's words. I really don't know what to expect next, because I have no idea what she's feeling, but I very cautiously step toward her and reach out my hand.

"Hey, do you think maybe we could go for a walk?"

To my complete shock, she doesn't angrily attempt to break my fingers; saying nothing, she rests her hand in mine.

Not waiting around to question her reasons, I squeeze her hand and start walking. Taking off my stiff, heel-cutting flats, I lead us toward the path, my bare feet finding comfort in its cool, well-worn dirt.

The full moon is higher now, and the sky is clear; the calm, black water sparkles brilliantly beneath it. But for once

I have no urge to grab my sketchbook, my pencils, and I guess maybe a flashlight or however I would do that in the dark. My mind is on other things. Obviously.

Counting on the perfect scenery to make me drunk enough to be bold, I open my mouth and try to say all the things Andrea had been too wounded to hear not that long ago. I tell her everything. That first meeting with Millie, when her psychotic driver of a brother had dropped her off and almost ran me over in the process; her idea of love that just *is*; how Bailey kept suggesting that we get together; the night Millie met Mom; Shapiro's symmetrical picture; the hand-holding; the kiss.

I hold nothing back, because I have nothing to lose.

I confess that Millie has taught me about love and quickly add that I absolutely do not love her. For such a smart girl, she has oddly simplistic conceptions of what love is—that shadow girl in her dreams, that girl from Millie's favorite book who was ready to love an Amazon just because she did. To me, love had been this monumental, scary thing because it meant I had one foot in the real world and couldn't just float off into my own world whenever I wanted. Being with Andrea had sort of forced me to be real, and I did not like that.

But then I kissed Millie and realized that she was right about love. I was attracted to her because, up until that point, she wasn't real. That moment had realized her for me. When she'd just arrived, my choice seemed to be between a real girl who had real feelings for me and an abstract ideal who let me escape that. But when it came down to choosing between two real girls with two hearts that could easily be broken, the choice became clearer.

I am like that girl in *The Arcadia*. It doesn't matter now, but I love Andrea because I do. And I'm just going to have to deal with that.

After emptying the contents of my brain, I take a long

breath. Then I cautiously joke, "Of course, the Amazon in the story was a guy in disguise, so it's a little off. Also, even if the girl was in love with a real Amazon, it'd still be a little off."

Andrea looks up at me, still frowning a little.

I force a laugh, hoping for a change in tone now that all the hard stuff has been said, "Well, uh, have you met you? You're basically an anti-Amazon in every way."

She does not laugh at my joke.

We walk a little farther. Then she stops and mumbles at the ground, "You're stupid, and I'm still mad at you."

That statement, devoid of any hint of humor as it is, invites a heavy, oppressive silence to descend between us. As if any words I could say now, any last-resort attempts to get her to forgive me would be crushed by it anyway. So I say nothing.

Then suddenly, she takes a step toward me and buries her face in my dress. Her arms are still hanging loosely by her sides, which doesn't encourage me into thinking that this is supposed to be some kind of intimate moment, but I put my arms around her and squeeze anyway.

She hugs me back, then looks up at the sky and screams. No words, just a loud, sharp yelp that sort of convinces me this night has been too much for her and she's lost her mind.

Then suddenly she meets my eyes. Her eyes are bloodshot; her whole face droops with exhaustion. Yet she's smiling. "Argh, I'm supposed to stay mad at you! What you did was so callous and mean, but I just—I keep coming back to seeing this whole night the way you must see it in your totally-out-of-touch Moira bubble. Like, you probably just kissed Millie because you were totally drunk on the scenery that night! If I'd been conscious, maybe you'd even have kissed me instead! And I know you spent lots of time after that night downing gallons of tea and having anxious fits every few minutes because you felt guilty. See, I think of it

that way and I'm not that mad, even though I should be."
She slaps my thigh for effect. "I'm messed up."

"You aren't messed up," I assure her, resting my chin
gently on her forehead. "You're wonderful and I love you,
even though I probably don't deserve you."

For a few seconds, she makes no sound at all. But soon
enough she makes a tiny chuckle, which turns into a sort of
rippling giggle, and then finally a full-on possibly insane
laugh as she attempts to stand on her tiptoes. Assuming she'd
intended to kiss me, I lean down to meet her, and feel the
tears on her cheek.

When she sinks back to the ground without doing
anything, I understand. Things can't just get better all of a
sudden.

But then she does it again. Hoping for something more
definite this time, I wrap my arms around her bony hips, then
lift her off the ground to my eye level. She entirely ignores
the suddenness of that and just kisses me lightly, then rests
her forehead on my nose as she whispers, "Moira, I just—I
love you too."

Resisting the urge to drop her in surprise, I squeeze her
tightly, then set her gently back on the ground. "Oh."

"What do you mean, 'oh'?"

"Haven't you been paying attention? The way things
were going, I assumed you were going to break up with me
by the end of the night! I figured you said those nice things
to soften the eventual blow because you're very professional
like that!"

"Come on, I was mad and hurt. I guess I'm still a bit hurt,
but I *saw* Millie's face. I've been rejected by enough girls to
know that she was telling the truth."

"Um, fine, but can I just point out that you've been
crying, like, this whole time? I figured you were sad because
you had to cut me loose, and you knew how hard I'd take it."

"Stupid." She giggles, with a sniff, "I don't even know

why I'm crying. Like, this night was supposed to perfect in my head. You'd show up looking gorgeous—which you did, by the way—and then we'd have a good time with our friends. Then I'd offer to walk you home. We'd have our moment on your doorstep where I told you I loved you, and you'd swoon because you were scenery drunk and felt the same."

There's another pause. Then I look into her eyes and say, "Telling you about Millie was not ideal, I know. But it did need to be said, and all of that other stuff sort of happened? Maybe not the porch thing, but I am feeling kind of scenery drunk and I do love you. Do you think I'd put myself through all this if I didn't? You know how afraid I am of conflict, and also reality! But it's all out there now, and I think I'll try to live in my bubble a little less after this. So, uh, maybe our perfect evening can be salvaged? It's a broken kind of perfect now, but at least I—"

Andrea puts a finger against my lips. "You're rambling. Shut up."

"I was just trying to suggest that maybe—"

With a strength that I didn't think her tiny self was capable of, Andrea pulls me to her eye level and gives me a long, forceful, passionate kiss. She then pulls back and takes a breath.

So maybe this night hasn't been perfect. I told Andrea I loved her in the stupidest, most wrong way possible and nearly broke her heart.

All the same, I *did* tell her. And she feels the same. That's something.

However it happened, it's out there now. In the wide-open real world. Where my parents or my brother or my campers or Aidan Hanley or anyone in the world can know that I ended up falling in love with the tiny creep who stalked her way into visiting the set of my dad's TV show.

"Andrea," I breathe, with a stupid grin I can't keep away,

"I know you're probably still upset. But, I don't know. Do you think that maybe we could—?"

Clearly not getting it, she scrunches up her face. "Huh?"

I stare at her significantly. She still doesn't catch on. A second later, excitement drives me to grab her hand and lead her toward my house.

Our orange porch light is the only light still on. No doubt Mom is already asleep. Dad is probably still at the resort, and Rory will definitely be spending the rest of the evening at Lunaside, wanting to squeeze every last bit of fun out of his last official night as camp counselor.

"Oh," she breathes with sudden comprehension.

***

When we get to my room, I lead Andrea to my bed. Then I move on top of her and press my lips to hers, empowered by all the frustrated passion caused by all the stupid things I've done and all the stupid times I've messed up before now that have never really gone away.

I press myself into her and move my hands across the smooth surface of her shirt. Even though all I am doing is sort of rubbing Andrea's hips and chest gently while she's clothed, she stares at me with what I can only call aroused confusion.

"Moira," she whispers.

Without responding, I get up and turn off my lamp. My love drunkenness has made me brave, but maybe not so much that I've stopped being me.

Once the room is dark—with the only light in the room now the faint glimpse of the full moon from the small, square window beyond the foot of my bed—I carefully remove my dress and head back to the bed, making sure to get Andrea's attention before slipping under the covers.

Her response is immediate. She rolls out of the bed,

goofily crashing to the floor in the process. I watch her silhouette unceremoniously undress, tossing her clothes away haphazardly. That surely expensive shirt lands in a pile of dirty socks, but I sense she won't care. In what is only enough time for me to catch a glimpse of her slight figure in the moonlight, she's under the covers, wrapping herself up in me.

The feeling of our bodies touching for the first time, skin to skin, is surreal. We've spent enough time together, even occasionally in situations like this, that it shouldn't be that big of a deal. But it is. If I had to describe it, all I can say is that it kind of feels like I'm melting—like maybe we both are.

Like maybe right now it doesn't matter which one of us is the tall, shy, neurotic one and which one of us is the small, oblivious, nerdy one, or which one of us exasperates the other with her openness or which one of us almost broke the other's heart. In this moment, we've become one fluid presence. Just a river of hands and arms and lips and noses and ears and hair, and eventually quiet noises and laughter, then shouts, then a sound like a scream that maybe comes from one of us or both.

Then, just like that, we are separate again. My body goes limp, and I sink into my bed, the room filling with a grayish sort of light.

Andrea groans. "Moira... Wow. Where did you —? I mean... Wow."

I lean in and kiss her ear but have no response. For the first time in my life, my mind is thought free.

Maybe we'll have to consider doing this more often.

She continues, still speaking in a half-groan. "I see now what people mean about craving a cigarette after. Except you know what I could go for? A bowl of ice cream. Do you think your dad's got some gourmet stuff in the fridge?"

A giggle escapes my lips as I hit her in the face with

my pillow. This night has been a lot of things for me, has possibly been the most emotionally charged moment of my life. But it hasn't changed my feelings on my girlfriend's nasty ice cream habit.

Chapter Twenty

Millie opts to stay with her brother for a few days after camp ends. Part of that is probably because she needs to cool off. Officially, though, it's because Randy has been so good to her since she got kicked out, and until now she'd repaid him by spending all of her time at Lunaside.

She stays there for the weekend. On Sunday night, I get a text message.

Leaving tomorrow @ noon. Would like to say goodbye; will understand if you can't.

So it ends up that I'm standing on the dock with Millie around eleven the next morning. I make sure to let Andrea know beforehand. She sarcastically tells me to try not to kiss her, but she's having brunch at the resort with her mother anyway and thus can't join me to supervise.

I'm supposed to meet her there when I'm done. That's because, as crazy and unlike me as it sounds, we have big plans.

The day is hazy. It's warm, too—warmer than any end-of-August afternoon has any right to be. The sky is filled with those mediocre, smoke-gray clouds that tease thunderstorms but never amount to anything exciting.

We fill the time chatting about the heat, until Millie blurts, "I called Mom last night."

"Whoa, how did that go?" I ask.

"Heh, not bad. She said I'm still kicked out until I get

over my 'phase,' but she didn't hang up immediately. She asked how camp went, if I'm going back to school and stuff. I told her I'm staying with a friend from school for now. In a week or so, Randy's going to help me go apartment hunting, even though I wouldn't need to do that if I was still living at home. She said 'That's good,' and that was pretty much it."

She smiles weakly, staring out at the water. "So things aren't fantastic. But they're okay. I'm safe."

"That's good," I reply, unsure of what else to say.

When the small ferry makes its way toward the old wooden dock that really doesn't seem fit to receive boats, Millie laughs her little nervous laugh and says something I don't think I hear right.

I think she says, "Thanks for this summer, Moira."

"I'm sorry, what?" I ask in disbelief.

She laughs. "Heh, I said thank you. And I meant it too. And I swear I haven't lost my mind."

I chuckle. "Okay, but seriously?"

When the ferry's passengers—all elderly people with loud shirts and khaki shorts—start disembarking, Millie watches them intently.

"Does any first love go anywhere?" she asks.

Not entirely sure if that question is rhetorical or not, I say nothing.

Eventually, she turns around and meets my eyes. She looks like she might cry, but she's also smiling. "Like, I made this huge deal about coming out to my parents. And, well, I guess it turned out to be, but all this stuff this summer, with you—I don't know, it made it all more real. And that was kind of medicine for me, 'cause I pretty much live in my head 24/7. Know what I mean?"

"Actually, I think I do."

Once the ferry starts boarding, she holds out her hand for me to shake. When I do, she pulls me into a hug.

"You gotta think of things my way. Remember what I

told you about Sidney? Guy's like my hero, and now I've got my own untouchable love to get me writing actual stuff, like he did. I promise not to write over a hundred poems and songs about you, though. Plus," she adds with a wink, "now I've got a tragic love story to charm future girlfriends. I'll be lighting up the dating scene from here on out."

I laugh.

After everyone else gets on, she picks up her duffel bag and clutches her wheeled suitcase. "So, yeah... See ya, Moira."

"Bye, Millie," I answer.

***

Andrea is waiting for me in front of the resort when I get there. Her khaki shorts and white polo shirt make her look like she belongs among the retirees, which makes me smile. When she notices me, she waves her keys in the air and yells, "Hey!"

I grin. "Hi!"

"Are you sure you're ready for this?" Andrea frowns. "I mean, when's the last time you left the island?"

I bite my lip. "Uh, well, never?"

On Saturday, while Andrea and I were relaxing on the dune, I'd gotten the bright idea to take her phone and start looking up art schools, just for fun. The satisfaction I'd gotten from the last couple of weeks of camp stuck with me. It was like in the process of helping my campers reach their goals, I finally realized that maybe I had those too. I still don't exactly know where I want to be in five years, but I at least feel like maybe I want to be *somewhere*.

One of the schools I found is close to the condo on the mainland that Andrea shares with her mother. And it isn't far from where Andrea is planning on going to school. Far enough that afternoon lunch dates won't be a regular thing, but she's not the type to sacrifice work for love anyway. Still, I am starting to feel like I can live with that. Spending basically every morning and evening with her is good enough for me.

That isn't exactly why I e-mailed the school and asked if I could do a tour, though. Really, the school seems like a solid fit for me. The website's former-student gallery has a lot of examples of people who do life drawing. Okay, so there is a pretty strong focus on nude models, but I'll just have to have that talk with Andrea if I get in.

So today we're hopping into Andrea's car and heading to the mainland to check this place out and see if it might be worth it to apply.

Doing this is world-shaking for me. Up until very recently, my world has been this tiny, closed-off space. If I left my room for any reason, it was usually to travel to some fixed point halfway down the path beyond my house—the dune, the resort, Lunaside. Never farther.

Now I want that world shattered, splintered, exploded. While I am still in love with Trundle Island, there is a slight chance that it isn't enough to hold me anymore. The me that is only now stepping out of the bubble I'd trapped myself in for so long needs a bit more legroom, I think. Not unlike the me I am when sitting in Andrea's car.

That I also have an adorable girlfriend who loves me, who will be ready to hold my hand and guide me through this new... whatever I am stepping into, simply because she loves me, only makes it more exciting.

And I guess a bit safer. Because however changed and matured by all the stuff that happened this summer I might be, I am still me, after all.

I grab Andrea's hands and look into her eyes. "I'm ready. If this summer's taught me anything, it's that maybe Mom knew what she was talking about. I should be at least thinking about schools. And possibly also living with you."

She smiles. "I can't wait to check it out with you! Also, Mom's having Aidan and Shapiro over for an end-of-summer party at our house here on the island, so the condo's going to be empty tonight."

"Huh," I reply, a sly smile creeping across my face. "You think maybe we could give living together a test run?"

Andrea looks at me and laughs as she unlocks the doors to her miniature excuse for a car. "We can *definitely* do that."

END

Acknowledgements:

I'd like to first say thank you to the many campers and counselors at the summer camps where I have attended and worked. Without your stories inspiring me, I'm not sure this book would have ever happened.

Thanks also to my *Lunaside* critique team:

Curtis Gallant, for being Lunaside's real-life fashion guru; Evan Harding, for his peerless copy-editing and pivotal plotting advice; Louisa Iannaci, for discussing exploding rainbows and providing professional advice on artistic technique; Marika Kailaya, for debates regarding the merits of sweater vests versus sundresses; Stephanie Kozak, for tirelessly reading every draft until she started talking about the Lunaside crew like they were real people; and finally Scott Rauscher, for being the world's tallest sounding board.

And a special thank you to the Torquere/Prizm team for their support! Specifically to my editors, Jessica St. Ama and Jaymi for patiently answering my metric ton of questions and helping me make my story the best it could be, and to all the writers who helped me during this process!

Lastly I'd like to express my gratitude to my parents and my assortment of sisters for keeping me on track, and making sure I was telling the story I meant to tell.

Lunaside

CPSIA information can be obtained at www.ICGtesting.com
Printed in the USA
LVOW04s1504220615

443396LV00016B/865/P